# A BRUSH WITH A BILLIONAIRE

## A CLEAN BILLIONAIRE ROMANCE

### LORANA HOOPES

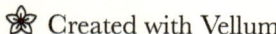 Created with Vellum

# DEDICATION

Dedication Page:

*To Melissa Storm who allowed me to write in the Sweet Grove kindle world while it was around.*

*To my friends who inspire me even when you don't know it.*

*To my wonderful readers who inspire me to write and keep writing even when it's hard.*

*To Jeanine Hawkins who encouraged me to write to market.*

# NOTE FROM THE AUTHOR

Thank you so much for picking up this book. If the beginning of this book seems familiar, it might be because you read it in the First Street Church Kindle World. It was originally a novella entitled Love Breaks Through. When the kindle world closed, Amazon gave us the rights back. I was just going to re-release it, but after reading it, I felt there was more to the story, so I added more and made it a full length novel. Even if you read the novella, there is much more to enjoy. I hope you enjoy the story and the characters as they are dear to my heart. If you do, please leave a review at your retailer. It really does make a difference because it lets people make an informed decision about books.

Sign up for Lorana Hoopes's newsletter and get her book, The Billionaire's Impromptu Bet, as a welcome gift. Get Started Now!

**Lorana's Other Billionaire Books:**

The Billionaire's Secret

The Billionaire's Christmas Miracle

The Billionaire's Cowboy Groom

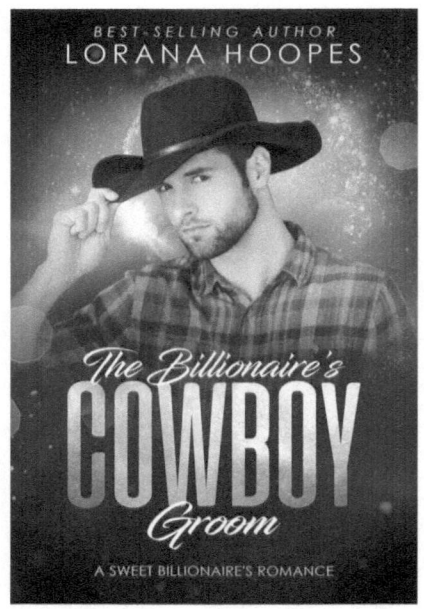

The Cowboy Billionaire coming soon

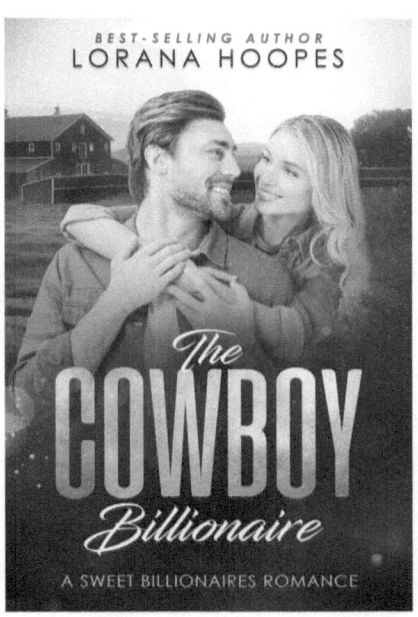

BEST-SELLING AUTHOR
LORANA HOOPES

*The*
# COWBOY
*Billionaire*

A SWEET BILLIONAIRES ROMANCE

# CHAPTER 1

*D*ING!

As Brent glanced at the display, a stream of curses tumbled out of his mouth. This was the last thing he needed. The check engine light gleamed, its orange glow mocking him for not taking the car into the shop last month for its regular inspection. Usually, he was a stickler for those things, but he had just finished filming a movie and his most recent breakup, Tricia, had been blowing up his phone since the breakup. It was only natural that a small thing like car maintenance had slipped his mind.

And the timing was impeccable, of course. The last major city was approximately ten miles back, and nothing but sagebrush passed by his window now. Dusty, dirty, yellow and brown sagebrush. Why had he thought going to a cabin in the middle of nowhere would help him relax? Oh, right, it had been Julia's idea.

Julia had been his agent for years, so he knew better than to argue with her when she told him he needed to get away and take some time to regroup. It hadn't really been his fault he lost it with the most recent director. The script had been terrible, and Brent was tired of roles that held no substance. But, he should have rented a cabin in the mountains or the penthouse of some nice hotel on the beach. With his money, he could have afforded either and been closer to humanity. But no, Julia had insisted a cabin out in the middle of nowhere would be preferable.

"Come on, baby," he urged the Porsche, hoping they had a good enough relationship she would get him to the next town. The size didn't even matter as long as it had a working phone. His cell phone had lost reception after the last big town. A mechanic wouldn't hurt either.

"Stella, if you get me to the next town, I promise I'll take you to the best shop when we return." Brent had named her Stella after the girl he had been dating at the time - a high maintenance ex-girlfriend. The girl, a penthouse owning, designer wearing, Tiffany's lover hadn't lasted, but the car had, until now.

His hands glided over the grey leather covered steering wheel, sending positive energy and good thoughts to Stella. Perhaps his touch would spur her to limp another two miles to… what was the name on the last sign? Soda Spurs? An odd name for a town, but in Podunk Texas, he expected no less.

But, it was not to be. With a final stutter and a plume

of blue smoke, Stella died on the side of Farm Market Road 1276. He glared at the asinine GPS that had recommended this shortcut in the first place and sighed. He should have stayed on the major highway. The city traffic was terrible, but at least a city would have guaranteed a tow truck and a mechanic in case of the unexpected. Now, he was stranded in the middle of nowhere with a hot, two-mile walk ahead of him.

As he popped the hood—hoping she had simply overheated and would work when she cooled down—more smoke billowed out from underneath. Brent was no mechanic, but smoke was never a good thing and probably meant a major fix. He checked the phone one more time in hopes the gods would show him pity, but it had no bars. *Useless!* It landed on the passenger seat as he swung open the car door.

The oppressive heat sent beads of sweat trickling down his back. Brent hated being sweaty unless he was at the gym. Even then, he always kept a towel close by. Salty stings in his eye while lifting heavy weights was not only annoying but dangerous.

He wiped a hand across his face before waving the smoke away and peering under the hood. A series of black and silver tubish things stared back at him, looking like a puzzle in a foreign language. He was not a car guy. Brent liked fancy cars – driving them, owning them, showing off in them, but he didn't care how they worked—that was why he paid other people. It was one of the many benefits of having money.

With a raised hand to shield his eyes, he scanned the road. Nothing but brown—unmoving, silent brown. A dirt plume at least would have meant a car was coming, but no dirt stirred along the road. He slammed the hood down.

With a heavy sigh, Brent snatched his worthless iPhone from the passenger seat, and jammed it back in his pocket. What good was having the latest technology if there were still parts of the state that had terrible service? Perhaps he needed to see about buying a few cell towers. There was a chance there would be cell reception in Soda Spurs though he doubted it.

He grabbed his laptop bag and then glanced into the backseat of the car to see if he needed to grab anything else, but there was nothing worth stealing there except his travel bag and it only held his clothes and toiletries.

A final thought urged him to grab the lukewarm bottle of water from the cup holder. His mouth turned down in disgust at the thought of swigging the warm liquid, but it was all he had.

After locking Stella, he flashed her one more longing glance, slung his bag over his shoulder, and began the trek. The dust from the road soon covered his expensive black loafers, turning them an ashy color. He would have to purchase new ones when he returned to civilization.

Sweat pasted his short dark hair to his head, and beads ran in little rivulets down his back and sides. Stains developed under his arms, and the heat coupled with the weight of the bag rolled his shoulders forward. He would be sore tomorrow, but he pushed on.

Relief flooded him as the first signs of life appeared. Small run-down houses dotted the side of the road. The faded paint on them crackled and curled, and the boarded windows kept their secrets locked inside. His gold Rolex told him he had been walking for eighteen minutes though it felt much longer.

Another few minutes yielded a green sign welcoming him to Soda Spurs, TX. Population 5003. *5003?* He sighed, certain that many people lived in a city block alone in Houston, but the houses looked a little newer, not expensive, but more cared for, which ignited a small sliver of hope. Newer paint and open windows allowed the light breeze to flow in and rustle the curtains.

He approached a blue house with white trim where a lone figure rocked in a chair on the porch. The gray of her hair suggested an elderly age, but her hands nimbly moved the needles she worked as the chair tilted forward and back. It emitted an odd creaking sound in the silence of the street.

"Excuse me, ma'am." Brent poured out the charm his mother had taught him to use at a young age. He didn't have to use it as much now as people flocked to him because of his money, but he could still whip it out when necessary. "Can you tell me where I might find a phone or mechanic?"

She frowned at him, wrinkles crisscrossing her face, though the beauty underneath was still visible. In her youth, she must have broken hearts left and right. Her hands slowed as her eyes narrowed. Perhaps his charm had lost its touch, or else maybe his ragged appearance was causing her concern.

"I don't mean to scare you, ma'am. My car broke down about two miles back, and I had to walk. Is there anyone in this town who can help me? A mechanic or a tow place or something."

The stare continued another long minute before his answer seemed to satisfy her, and she leaned back in her rocker, needles clicking again. "Sam's auto shop is up the way. Turn left at the gnarled tree." Her leathery hand pointed to the right. "Norma's is on the way. She'll give you a bite to eat if you stop in. Tell her Fanny sent you."

Her head dropped back to whatever she was making in her lap, and the rocker began its rhythmic motion again. Brent raised his hand in a thank you, wishing he had a cowboy hat to tip her direction. He hadn't worn one in ages, not since leaving the small town he grew up in, but an image of his mother flustered and blushing as a man tipped his hat at her flashed into his mind. The cowboy hat held a mysterious power over some Texas women, and it would have come in handy now.

Brent continued his trek, sighing in relief when a white building on the left caught his eye. It was more like a house than a business as only the small sign spelling

Norma's in faded red letters above the door informed him this was the restaurant. Three cars filled spaces around the house. A glance around revealed no gnarled tree so he turned into Norma's, hoping for better directions.

The cooler air smacked him as the door opened, sending a shiver racing along his spine. Two red booths and matching tables with red chairs filled most of the real estate in the room, which appeared to have once served as a dining room and living room.

The appearance outside had been deceptive as the inside was larger than he expected. Four stools, also upholstered in red fabric, sat in front of a large wooden bar. Rows of clear glasses lined several shelves behind the bar, and a drink dispenser that advertised Mr. Pibb and Mellow Yellow took up part of one wall. A cash register, the only newer contraption in the place, sat on the edge of the counter. At the far end of the room, a jukebox belted out an old country tune. Brent felt like he had traveled back in time.

All eyes in the place turned to him as the floor creaked beneath his feet, announcing his arrival. The room was not crowded. A man sat at the bar and a younger couple filled one booth. His eyes scanned the place, searching for the owner.

An older woman with short brown hair stepped out of the doorway he assumed led to the kitchen. A white towel was slung over her shoulder, and an apron, stained with many colors, hung on her waist.

"Can I help you?" she asked, wiping her hands on the apron.

"Yes ma'am. My car broke down a few miles outside town. I'm hoping you have a phone I can use as I can't get reception either." He pasted his best smile across his face —the one that got him any woman he wanted back home.

"Ain't got no phone, no use for one. Everyone here knows to come by if they need me." The woman shook her head once before turning back toward the kitchen.

"Wait." He stepped forward, his hand held out to her, though not too high. No sense in broadcasting his sweat stains. "I met Fanny, and she told me to find Norma. She also mentioned maybe Sam's shop could help get my car fixed."

Three pairs of eyes shifted from Brent back to the woman as if watching a slow-motion tennis match on TV.

A small grin tugged at Norma's lips as she turned back. "Well, if Fanny sent you, you must be all right. Why don't you sit, and I'll get you something to eat?"

He had eaten in the last town. At a nice restaurant. With servers who wore black pants and white shirts and handed him a proper menu. The single sheet of paper kind attached to a hard background and filled with elegant writing. He doubted Norma's even had a menu or if it did, it would be one of those laminated atrocities that would make a sticky, suction sound as you pried it open.

The steak and salad at the restaurant had filled him up, but his stomach rumbled at the idea of food. Perhaps a dessert and a cold drink would hit the spot. Snagging an empty barstool, he collapsed in it and dropped his bag on the floor. "Do you have pie and iced tea, unsweetened?"

A tittering of laughter circled the room. "Do we have pie?" Norma asked placing her hands on her meaty hips. "Honey, we have apple pie, cherry pie, blueberry pie, pumpkin pie, and mincemeat pie." She ticked the names off on her fingers. "Norma is known for her pie. Though considering Soda Spurs was founded on an apple orchard, people say my apple pie is the best."

"You tell him, Norma," the man in the far corner shouted, lifting his fork in the air in salute.

"I'll have a slice of apple then." Brent had never liked fruit pies, but there was no way he would pick something else and risk offending the woman.

She disappeared into the kitchen and returned with a large slice of apple pie on a white china plate. Tiny wisps of steam rose from the combination of cold whip cream against the warm crust, and the aroma of apples and cinnamon reached his nose before she even set the plate in front of him. Based on the smell, he feared the taste would be overpowering. A small silver fork appeared next to the plate, and then Norma stepped back, crossed her arms, and waited.

A furtive glance around revealed everyone in the room watching him. Nothing like tasting something with an audience hanging on your every move. He hoped it either would be fantastic or that he'd be able to maintain a poker face if it didn't, for he believed they would throw him out if he showed any dislike for the pie. It was almost as if a stranger's acceptance among this group hung on his or her reaction to the pie.

The fork slid through the dessert, and he raised it to his mouth. As the small portion hit his tongue, a burst of flavors exploded in his mouth. It was the best apple pie he'd ever had, and his eyes widened in surprise. Cheers and clapping ensued as his lips turned up and he nodded before taking another bite. His reaction seemed to have appeased Norma as she then filled a cup with cold iced tea for him. Brent took a few long gulps before placing the cup back down. His throat felt as arid as the Sahara, but the cool liquid did its job.

"So, Fanny mentioned Sam's. Is it much farther?" he asked between bites. He would regret finishing this pie the next time he hit the gym, but for now he didn't care.

"Nah, it's jest a little ways up past the gnarled tree," the man to his right said. His denim overalls stretched across his large frame and a plain white t-shirt with visible sweat stains poked out. Day old stubble covered his face, and his hair was brown but thinning on top.

"Does it have a street name?"

"I reckon, but no one round here uses it, so I can't rightly say I remember what it is." He picked up a toothpick and chewed on it.

"Don't mind Paul here." Norma shot a look at the stout man. "This is the outskirts of Soda Spurs. The main town has street names. Sam's is about a block up. If you get to Willow Street, you've gone too far."

"Thanks." He downed another gulp of tea and pushed the cleaned plate toward her. "How much do I owe you?"

Her hand flicked in dismissal. "First one's on the house. I can't have you passing out from hunger and dehydration. Marnie and Ernest would have my hide."

Another laugh erupted, and Brent forced a smile though he didn't understand what she meant. However, he knew from experience that small towns held many inside jokes.

"Well, thank you again." His legs buckled as he stood and he had to grip the counter to remain standing. They were still a little rubbery from the long walk. The reprieve had been nice. When all the feeling came back into them, he raised his hand in a wave, shouldered his bag again, and headed out the door.

Scorching heat beat down on him again as he stepped out of the air-conditioned diner, and his shoulder protested the weight of his bag. The reprieve had been nice. He should have asked for a bottle of water, but it had sounded like this Sam's place wasn't much farther. Perhaps, he would have water.

As the gnarled tree came into view, Brent could see why they used it as a marker. It was grey and twisted as if cursed with some ancient magic, and nothing was around it. There was no street sign marker, so if it had a name, it was keeping it secret.

Down this street were a few houses, painted in tans and beiges. They almost blended into the background. Up ahead, the small converted shop appeared among the neighborhood houses. He couldn't imagine the shop could hold more than one car at a time, but it probably didn't need to. He hadn't heard or seen a car driving in this town.

S A M' S was stenciled across the front door. As he pushed open the door, a bell jingled above his head announcing his arrival.

No one manned the cluttered counter, so he stepped into the large opening that led to the shop to the left. An old green Ford truck filled the space, and at the front of the truck, he spied two denim legs.

"Hello?" he asked. "I'm looking for Sam."

The legs rolled out from under the car until the full person was exposed. His heart stalled in his chest. Sam was not the greasy male mechanic he expected, but a petite brunette, though she was sporting a grease smear across her cheek. Her dark blue jumpsuit was large and hung on her body, hiding the curves he imagined lay underneath.

"I'm Sam. What can I do for you?" She wiped her hand on a red towel she pulled from her pocket as she met his gaze. Her blue eyes reminded him of the sky when no clouds filled it.

"But … you're a woman." The shocked words spilled out of his mouth before he could stop them.

Her eyebrow inched up her forehead as her arms crossed and leaned back. "Yeah, I'm a woman. You got a problem with that?"

He did, on so many levels. A woman could not possibly fix his Porsche, but he'd already ruffled her feathers. If nothing else, perhaps she would order whatever part he needed, and recommend a real mechanic.

Brent swallowed his pride and issued a lackluster apology. "No, I'm sorry. It's … I was expecting a man." Her sky-blue eyes continued to glare at him, waiting for a better explanation. "My car broke down outside of town, and I was hoping you could fix it or order a part or something."

Her gaze traveled the length of his body as if sizing him up. "What kind of car?"

"Porsche 911."

A snort escaped her mouth. "Figures."

Irritation flared within him. "I beg your pardon?"

"Figures you would drive such an uppity car. I could tell by the way you're dressed."

He bit his tongue to keep the reply he wanted to spew back at her in check. A few hasty generalizations on her outfit and the fact that she lived in this small town flooded his mind, but he needed her help. With great effort, he swallowed the vinegar and opted to pour out honey instead.

"You got me. I live in Houston, but I was hoping to get

away from the noise and relax. Can you help me?" He flashed his best puppy dog eyes at her, hoping they would work as well on her as they had on other women.

"Fine. I'll look at your snobby car. Follow me."

With a quick spin, she led the way through a back door where a faded blue Chevy truck waited.

# CHAPTER 2

Sam rolled her eyes as she climbed in the truck. The last thing she needed was a rich snob looking down on her, but she could use the money. She hadn't realized how hard it would be to open up her own shop. She should have rented a place closer to downtown, but she liked being away from the main buzz, and the building had been cheaper here. It was the cost of the renovation and all the equipment that had sucked her savings dry.

"Where are we going?" she asked as he climbed into the seat beside her. His head swiveled left and right eliciting a smirk from Sam. "There's no seatbelt, but I'll drive safe, don't worry."

"I wasn't worried," he sputtered, his forehead wrinkling as his brows knitted together. "Go back out the Farm Road. I'm about two miles outside town."

She nodded, and after putting the truck in gear, she pulled out onto the street. "What did you say you do again?"

"I didn't, but I'm an actor. Maybe you've heard of me. Brent McKasson?" The pride was unmistakable in his voice, and his chest puffed out as he spoke.

"Nope, but I don't watch much TV. I've got actual work to do."

"I'm a movie actor," he mumbled under his breath, clearly stunned she did not recognize him.

"Not here you're not. You're a big city name passing through. At least I assume you're not staying." She shot him a glance out of the corner of her eye to gauge his reaction.

"Only until my car is fixed."

Relief flooded her. "Well, in Soda Spurs, time moves a little slower. People are less hung up on money and fame, so don't be too disappointed if no one knows who you are. Besides, don't actors usually live in Los Angeles?"

"I guess some do. I prefer having a little more privacy, and I can fly wherever I need to be for filming. There."

She followed the direction his finger was pointing and smirked as the red Porsche 911 came into view. *It would be red*. Sam braked the truck beside the sporty car and turned off the ignition. "Did the engine smoke? Make any sounds?" she asked as she climbed down.

"Um, the check engine light came on and then smoke billowed out."

"What color? Can I have the keys?"

He handed them over, and she unlocked the car and popped the hood.

"What color what?" he asked, confused.

"What color smoke?" She backed out the driver's side and moseyed to the back of the car where the engine was located. "Was it white? Blue? Grey?"

"Does that matter? It was smoke."

"Yes, it matters." Irritation filled her veins as the hood flew up and she peered inside. She pushed the yellow tube to the side and peeked behind the engine. No oil appeared to be leaking, but sometimes a small leak was harder to see. After a few more pokes and prods, she slammed the hood down. "Well, it could be your AOS. That would be your best bet. The part isn't expensive, but it's a pain to get to, and I don't carry it. If that's not the problem though, then you probably blew your engine, and that's about a twelve-thousand-dollar fix."

His face paled as he blinked at her. "Twelve thousand dollars?"

"Yep, and I don't do them here," — she crossed her arms and stared at him — "so you'd have to get your car into a Porsche shop to have the repair done. However, if it's your AOS, I can replace it for you, but I won't know for sure until we get the car back to my shop."

"How do we do that? You have a tow truck around here?"

She held up a finger in a "give me a minute gesture"

and walked to the back of her truck. A long silver chain with a hook lay coiled in the bed. "We do it the old-fashioned way." Sam held up the hook and flashed a crooked grin as she stepped back toward the car.

"What? No way. You can't put that on Stella. The metal will scratch her paint." He stepped in front of Sam, halting her approach.

"You named your car Stella?" For some reason, she found the fact endearing. It made him a smidge more likeable, but only a smidge. Everything else about him grated on her nerves.

He shrugged but didn't budge.

Sam sighed and softened her tone as she returned his gaze. "Do you have a better idea? I don't have a tow service. Soda Spurs doesn't have a tow service. You can't drive her and even if you could, another two miles would blow the engine for sure."

Brent's eyes flicked from her to the car and back as he debated. Actual pain registered on his face when he answered, which made her smile. "Okay, fine, but please try not to scratch her."

"I'll do my best." Sam shook her head as she bent down to attach the hook underneath the car. Rich people were so hung up on their possessions they often missed the people around them. Though there were parts of the city she missed, that wasn't one of them.

As the hook clicked against the metal, Sam pushed the thoughts of the past from her mind. She dusted off her hands and faced Brent. "That should do it. I'll drive the truck back and you should steer the car, in case she slides. Hit the brakes only if necessary or you'll need a new bumper too."

"I can't believe I'm letting you do this," he grumbled under his breath as he got in the car.

Sam rolled her eyes as she climbed back in the truck. So much for him being likeable. She didn't miss people like Brent "what's his name" behind her, but she missed the opportunity sometimes. Her shop back in Dallas had been thriving. *No, I won't travel down that road again.* That door was closed. She needed to focus on making a living here.

The drive was slow, and she waved at Fanny, still sitting on her porch, as they passed. Sam wondered if Fanny did anything besides knit all day. At her age, there wasn't much else she could do, yet somehow, she knew everything happening, even on the outskirts of town.

When she arrived back at the garage, Sam parked on the street outside and shut off the engine. It would be too hard to tow the car inside and get it situated, so they would need to push the vehicle the rest of the way.

"You're leaving her here?" The incredulity in his voice carried with his volume as he stepped out of the car.

"No, I'm not leaving her here," — It took all her effort not to bite the man's head off — "but I didn't want to risk damaging her by trying to back in, so we will push her inside."

"I'm sorry, but we will do what?" He blinked at her as if she had spoken in a foreign language. Although looking at his dress, she might have. He had probably never done manual labor in his life.

"Push her." Sam stated the words slowly and with a mocking tone, stretching them to four syllables instead of the normal two.

His lips mashed together, forming a tight line, and she could almost see steam rising from his head. "I don't push cars."

An unattractive snort escaped her lips. "Well, you do today if you want me to look at her. I can't very well work on her in the street. You take the driver side and I'll take the passenger side. Put her in neutral and we'll push. It's not that hard."

With a final dirty glance her direction, he climbed back in the car and placed her in neutral. Then he stepped out, leaving his right shoulder under the frame. Sam opened the passenger door and braced herself for the coming weight.

It took them a bit to get the car moving, but once it did, they had it in place a few minutes later.

"Okay." Sam shut the passenger door and wiped a bead of sweat from her head. "I'll look at her and tell you what I think. If it's the AOS, I'll place an order and we should have it Monday. After I get it installed, we'll see if that's the whole issue or if it will need more attention."

"Monday?" Brent asked. "It's Friday. Where am I supposed to stay for a few days?"

Sam shrugged. Why did he think this quandary was her problem? "There's a bed-and-breakfast in town, but it might not have any rooms. Cowboy Shootout is this weekend."

"What?"

"Cowboy Shootout. A group comes through and re-enacts cowboy shootouts throughout downtown. There's a huge festival that goes along with it too including bobbing for apples—since that is our trademark here—hayrides, pie eating contest, you name it."

"Sounds fantastic."

Sam did not miss the sarcasm dripping from his voice. "Let me guess. You need a lift."

Brent shrugged his shoulders and offered an apologetic look.

"Fine, come on."

He grabbed his travel bag out of the car before joining Sam in the truck again.

As she drove through downtown, he faced the window, taking in the buildings. "They're all so small." The tone in his voice held a mixture of derision and disbelief.

"Yep, welcome to small town USA, where neighbors know each other's names and people at the grocery store remember what you buy because there's only two stores in town."

He mumbled something under his breath that sounded

like "I remember," but it was so quiet that Sam wasn't sure she'd heard him right.

As Soda Spurs Inn came into view, Sam released her breath, thankful Brent would no longer be her problem, but on top of the sign out front was a smaller one that read 'All Filled Up.'

"Great, what do I do now?" Brent asked, running a hand through his hair.

"Well, the other option isn't as nice, but Fanny has let a passerby stay with her occasionally. She's picky about who she lets stay, so you better put away your city boy attitude and see if you can find some small-town goodness."

"I think I can handle that." Brent shot her a pointed look. "I was born in a small town. What's your beef with the city, anyway?"

Sam shrugged, not wanting to divulge that shameful part of her past. "Nothing, I just knew too many people interested in the latest model rather than the reliable one."

He looked at her, his head tilted as if he wanted to ask another question but decided against it.

A few minutes later, they arrived back at Fanny's. She was in her usual position on the porch, rocking back and forth. Brent's posture stiffened beside her.

"Are you nervous? Talking to a little old lady?" Sam couldn't help but laugh.

"If she says no, I have no place to stay, so yeah, the stakes are a little high, and I wish I had a hat."

Sam furrowed her brow, not understanding what a hat would change, but not caring enough to ask a clarifying question. "Come on, it will be fine." After shutting the door behind her, she sauntered up to the porch. "Hey, Fanny."

"Hey yourself, Sam. I see you met our friend." Fanny glanced at Brent without missing a stitch in her knitting.

"Sure did. He will be here a few days while we wait for a part and Soda Spurs Inn is full due to the festival." Sam shoved her hands in her pockets. "Any chance you have a free room?"

Fanny turned her eyes on Sam and paused her needles. Then she glanced at Brent. Sam followed Fanny's eyes to Brent who stood with a small, hopeful smile on his face. "Sorry, I'm filled up too." Brent's expression faltered, but Fanny continued. "Don't you have an extra room at your place, Sam?"

Sam's head whipped back to Fanny and she stuttered over her words. "Fanny, that wouldn't be proper." A quick glance at Brent revealed the same shock on his face. There was no way she wanted the chauvinistic city-boy in her extra room and invading her space.

"I see it as being neighborly. It's only for a few days." Fanny raised an eyebrow at Sam. "He has nowhere else, right?"

Sam opened her mouth to speak but shut it and sighed instead. Fanny was right. Brent had nowhere to stay if she didn't open her house, and though her mother was gone, she would have had Sam's hide if she turned her back on someone who needed help.

She turned to Brent and forced the words past gritted teeth. "Fine, you can stay with me, but only for a few days."

"No worries," he said, holding up his hands. "I don't plan to be here any longer than necessary."

"Come on. Thanks, Fanny, we'll see you around."

"I'm sure you will." As the old woman smiled and resumed her knitting, Sam wondered about the gleam in her eyes.

# CHAPTER 3

*S*am pulled the truck up to a small rambler with peeling beige paint and a lawn in need of serious maintenance. Brent glanced at her out of the corner of his eye as he exited the vehicle. For as knowledgeable as she appeared about cars, she must not be much of a home maintenance expert. Neither was he, but that's why he had a penthouse apartment. No yard to worry about.

He followed her up two creaking porch steps that sagged under his weight. How had she never fixed these? They felt as if they'd succumb any day.

She shoved the key in the lock and turned his direction, indecision flooding her eyes. He knew she didn't want him here, but he didn't want to be here either. He wanted to be in the peaceful cabin ignoring the press and contemplating his future.

He had made the majority of his money playing the Night Ranger, but it was getting old, and he wanted something that showed off his talent more. The only problem was he didn't know what that was.

The front door swung open, and Brent followed Sam into the simple living room. Two chairs and a couch, mismatched as if they came from Goodwill or the nearest garage sale, sat in the middle of the room. A scratched coffee table was situated in the center of them, cluttered with paper, but it was the three full bookshelves that garnered most of his attention.

He loved reading, but he rarely met people who read more than their scripts these days, and even fewer owned a book. Those who did read didn't use paperback books anymore; they downloaded them to their Kindle or other device, but Sam evidently had a penchant for the real thing. He found his opinion of her shifting. Anyone who still enjoyed a paperback had to have some redeeming qualities. Perhaps she was worth getting to know better. He wanted to peruse her shelves to see what she liked to read, but she spoke, diverting his attention first.

"The kitchen and dining room are here." She pointed to the right. "Use what you want, but the cupboards are bare. The market is on Willow street, and you can walk there. There's also a few restaurants—Marnie's on Madison, Ernesto's, and a few others, but they're farther in town."

She turned left down a narrow hallway and Brent

followed, his head spinning from the unfamiliar names she was spouting. The hallway walls were plain, white, and barren of pictures and personality. How long had she lived here? At the end of the hallway it split, and she headed left again, opening a door to a bedroom.

"This is the guest room. You can stay here. It's not much though."

Solid blue colors decorated the simple room. A full-size bed, dresser, and desk were the only furniture pieces, but it was better than no room.

"The bathroom is down the hall. I have my own, so we don't have to share. There's a towel on the rack you can use and extras in the hall closet across from it. My room is there," — she pointed to the closed door at the other end of the hall — "and it's off limits."

His eyebrow arched at the thought of invading her room. Clearly, she didn't know his type. Blond and chesty was what he preferred—at least after Rachel—not sassy and grungy. "I doubt you need to worry about that. My goal is to relax while I'm waiting for the part and then leave as soon as possible."

"Fine, I'll leave you to it then. I'm going back to the shop to inspect your car and order your part."

"Wait, do you get cell service here? Or do you have a phone? Just in case."

She raised an eyebrow at him. "Yes, you can get cell service here; we aren't that backward. And there's a phone in the kitchen if you need to use the landline."

Without another word, she spun and left him blinking in the hallway. He shook his head as he entered the guest room. While he appreciated the bed, her hospitality left a lot to be desired. Why did she seem to hate him so much? Granted, he had made a sexist comment when he first met her which he should apologize for, but her reaction seemed more intense than the comment called for. Was he giving off an unintentional vibe? He'd have to watch himself and see.

After tossing his bags on the bed, he opened his travel bag and pulled out the latest script. It was another Night Ranger movie. With a sigh, he sat on the bed and began reading. He only made it five pages before he tossed the script aside. Just like the last four movies, it was nonsense and drivel covered up with a lot of action and shirtless scenes. With a growl of frustration, he raked a hand through his dark brown hair and down his stubbled chin. He needed a shave and a shower. Perhaps the warm water would invigorate his senses and allow him to see it in a different light.

He rummaged in his bag for his travel kit. With it in hand, he walked down the hallway and flicked on the bathroom light revealing one sink, a toilet, and a bathtub. A blue hand towel hung near the sink and a matching larger one adorned a rack near the shower. The whole bathroom was smaller than most of his closets back home.

He placed his bag on the small counter housing the sink and removed his razor and soap, putting them on the shower shelf. Then he stepped into the tub, pulling the curtain closed before turning on the faucets. The warm water pelted his back, but he didn't mind. Brown trails streamed down his chest and swirled into the drain below. The dirt washing off felt good after his long walk into town.

When he finished the shower, he wrapped the towel around his waist, gathered his clothes and bag, and headed back to the room. He pulled on a pair of cargo shorts, forgoing the shirt for now, and resumed his position on the bed. Script in hand, he continued reading, but it was no use. Freshly showered or not, the script was still awful.

With a sigh, he dropped the script once more, grabbed a shirt, and decided to check out the rest of the house and the town. He would have to call Julia later and tell her to start looking for something else or else he would need a career change.

The fridge was as empty as Sam claimed. A bottle of ketchup, mustard, and a half empty milk carton were the only things on the shelves. A look in the cupboard revealed a few spices, pop tarts, and a few boxes of cereal. This woman was clearly not a cook.

He shut the cupboards and patted his pocket to make sure he had his wallet before heading to the front door, where he paused momentarily as he debated whether to lock the door or not. Since Sam had left him with no key and no return time, he opted to leave the door unlocked.

He didn't plan to be gone long, and the town seemed relatively safe.

He headed north, trying to remember Sam's directions, and took a left on Willow Street. Soon a market, sharing lot space with a gas station, came into view. The small shop was not his normal fare, but with a resigned sigh, he entered the store, grabbing a basket from a stack near the door.

Brent couldn't remember the last time he had been in a grocery store. Back in Houston, he had an assistant who shopped for him, and if he needed something while she was gone, he simply ordered it online and had it delivered.

The small store only held a handful of aisles, and after filling the plastic basket with meat, fruits, and vegetables, he checked out and retraced his steps back to Sam's place.

Back in her kitchen, he unpacked the groceries before inspecting the rest of the house. He was curious about this woman and headed to her bookshelves first.

Classics ranging from Wuthering Heights to Moby Dick filled several of the shelves. He hadn't taken her for a reader of books of old. A few self-help books were interspersed on the shelves, mainly on dealing with loss and rejection. Could that explain her emotional walls?

Turning from the bookshelves, he scanned the area, but no pictures hung in the living room either. Where were her photographs? Her art? His eyes landed on the messy coffee table, and he perched in the nearest chair, picking up the papers and scanning them.

Words and art were scrawled across them. Had he stumbled across her journal? A closer look revealed not a journal, but a verse across the top, followed by her thoughts and applications for it. Devotionals. These were her devotionals. He hadn't picked up a religious vibe from her, but then not everyone screamed their religion. Rachel never had either. She had just had this quiet peace about her, a welcoming countenance, and a kind word for everyone she met.

The papers fell from his hand as the image of Rachel flooded his mind. Focusing on Rachel would only make him sad.

# CHAPTER 4

Sam smelled the food before she opened the front door. The aroma of garlic, steak, and vegetables floated through the air, reminding her of home-cooked dinners before she left for trade school.

As she stepped into the living room, the sound of whistling and something sizzling in a skillet met her ears. Her keys clattered onto the table by the door before her feet carried her into the kitchen.

Brent stood with his back to her, stirring a pot on the stove. Remnants of cut up vegetables cluttered her bar. He turned, his whistling stopping in mid-note.

"Hello, I hope you're hungry because I've made dinner. Your cupboards were empty."

Sam blinked at him. Though her stomach rumbled, she was more confused at the image in front of her. She hadn't pegged him for a cook; employing a personal chef seemed more his style. "Um, yeah, I am," she muttered. "Let me go get cleaned up and I'll help."

"No need," he called after her. "It's done."

She shook her head as she walked to her room. When she'd agreed to this arrangement, she had expected he would stay hidden and she would rarely see him. A dinner date, informal as it was, had not been in her plan. Yet there he was, looking at home in her kitchen and handsome in his shorts and t-shirt.

Handsome? What was she thinking? Though she hoped to find love again one day, she had promised herself a long time ago she would never fall for another rich snob. Wasn't that why she moved to this town? To return to her roots? To simplicity?

Those thoughts ran through her head as she peeled off her grungy clothes and stepped into the shower. She had never been one to shy away from dirt, but she always enjoyed washing it away. To her, it represented cleansing her sins as the water ran over her and her fair skin re-emerged. She usually used the time to reflect on her day and ask forgiveness for areas she might need it, but tonight her thoughts remained on the man in her kitchen and the impending dinner.

After drying off, she pulled on a pair of shorts and her favorite London t-shirt. She had never been, but she'd long obsessed over the region. One day she'd save up enough to visit. Her fingers combed through her wet hair, fluffing it before she returned to the kitchen.

Brent had set her kitchen table and sat at the chair closest to the stove. Her heart fluttered at the image. How long since she'd enjoyed the company of a handsome man?

He glanced up at her, a smile on his perfectly formed lips. "Join me?" He pointed to the seat across from him.

"You didn't have to make dinner." Sam dropped her eyes as she pulled out the chair. What was this nervous sensation fluttering through her?

"That's true, but pop tarts didn't sound appealing or satisfying. How do you eat normally?"

"I usually grab something at Norma's on the way home. Since it's only me, it lasts me a few days. I'm surprised to see you cook. I figured you'd have a professional who cooked for you."

He cocked his head as he regarded her. "I do, but my late wife was a gourmet chef. She taught me a few things, and I wasn't always a well-paid actor. Before I landed my first big role, I was a starving author from a small town who had to do everything myself, and I kind of miss cooking."

Sam lowered her gaze. She should know better than to assume. "I'm sorry about your wife." She wanted to know more about his wife like how they met, how long they were married, and how she died, but those were personal questions, and she didn't know him well enough to be asking them.

"Thank you." His voice softened. "It's been a few years, but I still miss her."

Unsure of what else to say, Sam nodded and folded her hands to pray. In addition to thanking God for the food, she added a request for humility and understanding. When she opened her eyes, Brent was staring at her.

"How long have you been a believer?"

The question caught her off guard, but it didn't sound condescending, only curious. She inhaled a deep breath. "All my life, I guess. My parents were believers, and they took me to church every Sunday. I enjoyed it until I went to trade school and then I got ... distracted." She paused, biting the inside of her lip at the memory. "When my mom died, I realized I needed to get right with God again, so I moved here hoping a slower pace would help me focus."

Brent filled her plate with the meat and vegetables he had grilled up before speaking again. "I'm sorry about your mom."

"Thanks." Though he hadn't asked how, Sam could tell he wanted to just as she had wanted to. And while she didn't like talking about it, some tug in her heart told her she should. "She was killed by a drunk driver."

His hand paused in mid scoop, and his eyes locked with hers. A mix of brown and gold with tiny green flecks, they mesmerized her. He dropped his gaze, finished placing the vegetables on his plate, and ran a hand down his chin before meeting her gaze again. "How did you forgive God?"

With that question, she could tell he held a similar pain in his past, and she prayed for the words to say to reach him. "When I was little, my dog died, and it hit me hard. I wanted to blame God, but my mother told me about Jesus. She told me that God never meant for us to have sickness and pain in our life, but that when sin entered the world, it changed. However, God wanted to save us all, so He sent his son to Earth to die for our sins. When I realized that Jesus died for all of us, even though He had never sinned, I realized death was a part of life and God wasn't to blame, but He is there for us when tragedy strikes if we will reach out to Him."

She could see the muscles tensing in Brent's jaw as he mulled over her words. He opened his mouth to speak, but then closed it again and dropped his gaze to his plate.

The corner of her lip tugged upward. God must be working on his heart, and she was sure he'd have more questions when he was ready.

As she lifted her fork, she sniffed the appetizing food and her mouth watered. Norma was a good cook, but how long had it been since her last home cooked meal? The flavors created a symphony, and Sam wondered what other secret talents Brent possessed.

"You mentioned you were born in a small town," she said after swallowing her bite. "Which one?"

He shook his head and the corners of his lips turned

up. "Star Lake, Texas, and let me tell you nothing is there. We had one stoplight, and for entertainment, we would drive around the main square, called the drag, and check out the general store parking lot because that was the meeting spot. I think that's why I turned to writing. The boredom forced me to create worlds to keep me entertained."

"I can see that. I grew up in Junction West. I remember thinking there had to be more than this tiny town. I couldn't wait to get out, and I left for trade school as far away as possible while staying in the state. After Mom's death, the familiarity and camaraderie of a small town calmed me. I used the money I received from her will to open up the shop." She took another bite of the caramelized asparagus enjoying the conflicting flavors of salty and sweet.

"I noticed you have a lot of books. Are you a big reader?"

Sam smiled. "I enjoy reading, but those books were my mom's. She loved books of all kinds, but especially the classics. She would read to me every night before going to bed when I was young. When she died, my father told me he didn't want the memories reminding him of her every day, so he boxed them up and sent them all to me." She shrugged. "I haven't read many of them, but I enjoy the reminder of her."

Brent nodded. "I can understand that."

"So, you mentioned you were an author. Did you give it up for acting?"

"I didn't give it up entirely, but acting brought in more money. And becoming famous then helped with book sales, but I still write when I can."

She nodded. He had quite the busy past. "What type of movies do you act in? I have to warn you, I don't watch a lot of TV, and I can't remember the last time I went to a theater so I probably haven't seen them."

Brent laughed. "You probably wouldn't enjoy them. I do action movies mostly. Kind of like Mission Impossible - only in space."

"Oh," Sam tried to keep her tone neutral and failed miserably, "well, that sounds interesting."

"No, it's awful." Brent's laugh was rich and hearty, and it made little lines appear on the sides of his eyes. "The plots are terrible and the scripts..." He shook his head. "Don't even get me started on the scripts."

"So, why do you do them?" Sam asked.

"It wasn't what I wanted to do when I first moved to LA. I wanted to write amazing scripts with depth and character, but it's hard to get scripts looked at when you are unknown. So, I decided to get known, but like most struggling actors, I started doing commercials and low budget films. Then I met Rachel who was working in a restaurant. She had dreams of opening up her own restaurant, but we couldn't do that on what I was making, so when Julia approached me with the first Night Ranger movie and told me how much it paid, I took the audition. I figured I could make enough to help Rachel open a restaurant and maybe make a name for myself so I could get better roles and sell my books."

"And did you?" Sam asked intrigued.

"Make a name for myself? Yeah, but not the kind I wanted. The books started selling which was great, and about a fourth of my fortune comes from royalties. But the Night Ranger movie made so much money that they extended my contract for three more movies. Not only did they keep me busy, but I got pinned into that typecast. Now, I can't get anyone to take me seriously as they only see me as this shirtless GI Joe type character."

"I'm sorry." Sam had no idea how acting worked. She had always assumed it was an easy job that anyone could do. "How about the restaurant? Did Rachel get to open one?"

"Yeah, that's what moved us to Houston. She wanted to open it in a big city but away from the celebrity clientele. As I was from Texas originally, I didn't mind moving back, and by then I was making enough money to charter a plane to fly me to auditions or movie sets. Of course, now I'm no longer sure I want to keep acting. While the money is nice, I don't need it. I have more than I'll probably ever spend and the manager who runs Rachel's restaurant is amazing, so I make a passive income from that too. I can't keep doing something I dread, and if

I can't get a serious role, then it might be time to hang up my hat, as they say."

"What would you do if you didn't act?" Sam asked. "Would you go back to writing?" She found herself intrigued by all of Brent's layers. She had thought he was just a rich snob, but there was a lot more to him.

"Probably. It's a lot easier to sell books now that I'm a known name. And I'm sure I could write a decent script and get it sold now. I've read enough bad ones to at least know if mine was better."

"Whatever it is, I hope you find it."

Their eyes locked for a moment, and some unseen current passed between them. Afraid of what it might mean, Sam dropped her eyes to her plate and they finished dinner in silence.

When her plate was empty, she chanced looking at him again. "How about I do the dishes since you cooked?"

"No way." He shook his head. "You're letting me stay here while you fix my car; the least I can do is help with dishes."

"Suit yourself." She sent a smile his direction. Doing dishes was one of her least favorite chores, and she was happy not to have to do them alone for once. "Wash or dry?"

He brought the plates to her as she filled up the sink with water. "I'll wash."

"Good." With a laugh, she grabbed a nearby towel, "because I hate washing."

Sam didn't mind living alone most days, but one big drawback to it was having to do all the chores by herself. It was probably another reason she let Norma do most of her cooking.

With an experienced hand, he scrubbed the plates before handing them to her. She dried them, enjoying the companionable silence between them. As she turned to grab the next dish, something wet smacked across her face, sending her reeling back in surprise.

When Brent laughed, she realized he had splashed her with water. She whipped her towel at him in a playful gesture. "Not nice," but she smiled as she said it.

"Sorry, but I couldn't resist." His voice trailed off as their gazes locked.

Sam's heart thudded in her chest as unseen electricity crackled between them.

Brent reached up and wiped her nose. The trail his fingertips left flared with heat, and Sam knew if she didn't get out of the room, she would end up kissing Brent McKasson and there was no point in that. While he had proved he wasn't completely a snob, he still lived in a very different world than she did, and a relationship would never work.

"I should…" No good excuse came to her mind as conflicting emotions coursed through her body. "Bed. I should get to bed. Long day working on your car tomorrow." She hated that she was stammering over her words and even more that his twinkling eyes and twitching lips told her he knew he affected her. Before he could say anything else, she tossed the towel on the counter and hightailed it for the hallway. "Thank you for dinner," she said before turning down the hall.

"You're welcome," he called after her, and she could hear the laughter in his voice.

Sam entered her room and shut the door, leaning against it. What was happening with her? She was not normally star struck, and she'd promised herself she would never fall for another rich man. That had been easy when she thought Brent a snob, but then a different side of him had emerged. A side she somewhat liked. A side that scared her a little as it sent her heart fluttering in her chest.

# CHAPTER 5

*B*rent wandered into the guest bedroom. He should be reading through the latest script, but Sam's soulful blue eyes and the way her lips were a little off-kilter when she smiled clouded his vision.

He had expected she would sit down at the table, grease and all, but she had opted for a shower. And when she had returned and sat across from him, the scent of strawberries from her shampoo had tickled his nose. She cleaned up nicely, and with her hair down, her face exuded femininity.

Then she had shared the story of her mother. It was almost his story of losing Rachel to a tee. He even had Rachel's cross necklace on his nightstand back home to remind him like Sam had her mother's books. What were the chances of that? The only difference was he had blamed God. He had stopped going to church and started dating women he knew he'd never fall for because he hadn't wanted to get hurt again.

Sam's words rattled around in his head. Was she right? Had he been wasting time blaming God when he should have been thanking him for the time he'd had with Rachel?

An image of a man on his knees flooded his vision, and Brent grabbed his laptop from his bag. Could this be a story? He placed the computer on the desk and sat down. He hadn't expected to do any writing during this trip. It had just been about getting away from the public, but he wouldn't turn the writing time down. Though he had written often before the Night Ranger movies, he had put the pen aside when he'd found acting. Taking on characters had taken the place of creating characters.

However, as he placed his fingers on the keys, images flooded his mind. The story played out, almost like a movie in his head. With a huge intake of breath, he closed his eyes and let the story come. Image after image flooded his mind as the premise played out in pictures. When it paused, he opened his eyes and typed out the words as fast as possible.

Line after line, the words came, filling the screen. When the river of words ran dry, he stretched his shoulders, surprised to find them stiff. How long had he been writing? A glance at the clock showed three hours had passed. When was the last time he had written for such a lengthy stretch? A glance at his document showed four thousand words. He hadn't pounded out that many words in one sitting in ages.

As he stood from the chair, he reached his arms above his head and bent sideways to relieve the stiffness in his back. It was not done, but it was a start. He had no idea if it would go anywhere but the story needed to be told. He could feel that.

The hallway was dark as he headed into the bathroom to brush his teeth. Sam must already be asleep. He paused outside the entrance and stared at her closed door, wondering how she slept. Did she sleep on her back or on her side? Left or right side of the bed? Brent shook his head to dispel the thought. He was simply here for the weekend, nothing longer. Come Monday he'd continue to the cabin and then his life back in the city. He had no business thinking anything about Sam other than when she would fix his car.

∾

The scent of coffee woke Brent in the morning. He rubbed his eyes and stretched the kinks out of his neck. Though not the most comfortable bed, the exertion from the day had worn him out, and he had fallen asleep quickly.

He flicked the blanket aside, swung his legs out, and planted his feet on the carpeted floor. His own apartment back home had hardwood floors, and as much as he loved the look of them, he abhorred the chill that caressed his feet first thing in the morning. This soft, fuzzy carpet feeling was much nicer and definitely less jarring.

After pulling on a pair of jeans and a shirt, he wandered down the hallway toward the percolating coffee pot that held a promise of invigoration for the day.

Sam stood watching the brown liquid pour into a mug. Sweats hung low on her hips and a loose-fitting tee stopped shy of the waistband, displaying a hint of pale skin.

A trickle of desire flooded his veins, but he banished the thought. He was here for coffee, nothing more.

As he took another step, she turned. Even first thing in the morning, her charm radiated. Her pale skin was devoid of any makeup, but held a natural elegance, and he noticed a dusting of freckles across her nose that he hadn't observed before.

"Morning, did you sleep okay?" The coffee finished its cycle, and she picked up the mug, cradling it with her hands as if seeking its warmth.

"Not as nice as in my bed back home, but better than the backseat of my car." His bed back in Houston was a King-sized memory foam mattress covered in eight hundred thread count Egyptian sheets, but he felt no need to divulge that information.

Sam's lip twitched before pulling into a large grin. "Oh, speaking of which," —she pointed a finger his direction— "I got your part ordered, but since it was Friday, it won't arrive until Monday, even overnighted."

A feeling of relief flooded Brent. Even though he knew he and Sam traveled in different worlds, he wanted to spend more time with her. "Well, I guess that's all we can do." He cleared his throat and switched the topic. "Is there any more of that coffee?"

"Yep, cups are in the cabinet above the pot. I may not have much else, but I always have coffee."

She sat down at the small dining table as he turned to the cupboard and fished out a mug.

"Sugar?" he asked.

"No thanks, I'm good."

He turned to find her smirking up at him. "No, I mean where do you keep the sugar? I take two." She pointed to another cabinet and after pouring in the desired amount and stirring the dark liquid, he joined her at the table.

The silence pressed down on him until he couldn't stand it any longer. "You mentioned there was a festival in town this weekend?"

Her eyes flicked up, a mysterious glint sparkling in them. "Yep, the cowboy festival."

"Have you ever been?" He threw the question out and then dropped his eyes to his mug to give the impression he didn't really care.

She shook her head, sending a few tendrils of her chestnut hair flying and the smell of strawberries wafting his direction again. "No, I've only been here six months, so I wasn't here for it last year."

Ah, well that explained her lack of pictures on the wall. "Well, since you can't work on my car, would you care to attend? I could use it as character research, I mean." He added the last sentence hoping she wouldn't pick up on his eagerness to spend the day with her.

"I thought you stated you were an action star." Sam narrowed her eyes at him.

"I did." Brent shrugged, trying to appear nonchalant, "but I write too, remember? You never know when I might need to use the character development."

"Mmhm. You really want to attend a small-town festival?"

"I mean, if you want." He watched her face closely to see some sign, any sign of what she was thinking. Could she sense his interest? Did she return it?

Sam's eyes scanned his face before she sat back and crossed her arms. "Sure, why not?"

Nodding, he dropped his eyes to his mug again, and the silence descended once more, but the thrill of spending time with her sent his heart thudding, and he had to force the corners of his lips not to turn up in a smile.

~

*S*am was forced to park at the elementary school as barricades closed the streets from Main to Lonestar Avenue. As they approached the crowd, she waved to those who sent a greeting their direction.

"That's Heather Shelton. She's the pastor's daughter. And that's Rose Minor. She runs the Soda Spurs flower shop. Kind of ironic, don't you think?"

Brent nodded, trying to remember the names, but knowing he would fail.

A white table sat under a tent in front of the post office. Emblazoned in black across the banner that hung from the table were the words "Cowboy Shootout," and a younger man and a woman stood behind the table, cowboy hats on and fake guns hanging from holsters at their hips.

Brent and Sam joined the line.

"Howdy pardners." The woman greeted them when their turn arrived. "Will you be wanting to join the shootout or just the other festivities?"

Sam looked to Brent who shrugged. "Might as well try it all out, I guess."

The woman beamed. "Wonderful. The cost is thirty dollars per person."

Brent and Sam both reached for their pockets.

"I have this," Brent said.

"Not on your life," Sam retorted. "I can pay for myself."

The woman watched the exchange with a smirk and raised eyebrows. As both Sam and Brent put their respective money on the table, she scooped it up and continued her spiel. "The action begins at high noon. We're using paint ball type guns, but it's washable coloring. There's a booth in the post office where you can rent western gear or buy it if you want to keep it. The old-time photographer is set up at city hall, and the diner will serve beans and cornbread after the shootout. Connor here will be rounding everyone up at 11:30 on First and Main to go over the rules, so that gives you," — she glanced at her watch, the only anachronistic piece of her outfit — "about forty-five minutes."

She handed them a map which listed all the activities and where they would occur, and after thanking her, they headed to a shady area to take a closer look.

"What do you want to do first?" Sam asked.

"We should experience everything, so let's head over to the post office for outfits." He tried to sound casual, but the thought of dressing up as a cowboy with chaps and guns excited him. Visions of running around pretending to be a cowboy when he was younger flooded his mind.

Sam's eyebrow arched, but she shrugged and led the way.

The post office had closed early for the day, and a table displaying hats and belts of all colors sat in the small lobby. Two clothing racks filled the rest of the space. Colorful shirts, vests, and chaps hung from the metal rods. There were even gingham dresses, but Sam opted for the more masculine outfit and perused the shirts.

After flipping through the rack, Brent picked a solid blue shirt for himself, a black leather vest, matching chaps, and a hat. A small dressing area with curtains draped over PVC pipes sat snugly in the corner, but Brent offered the space to Sam, opting to put the western shirt over his tee.

When she emerged a few minutes later, his heart skipped a beat. The chaps were a little big, even cinched in, and hung on her hips. Her red shirt complemented the brown of her vest and chaps. She pushed the hat up with one finger and offered a crooked grin. "Is it awful?"

He shook his head, transfixed by the sight of her. The image was sexy, but he couldn't say that out loud.

Her smile broadened before she dropped her eyes. "We're all dressed up, what now?"

Brent checked his watch. They had twenty minutes left. "Want to take a picture? That way you can prove you got this rich boy to dress up?"

She laughed and swatted his arm. Her laugh was the sound of the wind chime he used to have on his back porch growing up, and his lips pulled into a smile of their own.

After exiting the post office, they raced across the street to City Hall. The atrium had been transformed into a makeshift photography studio. Huge lights surrounded a camera on a tripod.

"Welcome," the young woman behind the camera

greeted them as they approached. "Pick a prop from the table, and I'll be right with you."

Brent and Sam examined the table which housed glass bottles, fake shotguns, cards, ropes and fans. Sam grabbed the fake rifle which evoked another smile from Brent. Not being a drinker or a card player, he opted for the rope.

"Ah, perfect." The photographer pointed to two crates in the middle of a host of other props. "Sit, sit."

Brent sat on the right crate, hoping it would hold his weight, and Sam took the left one, draping the gun across her lap.

"No, no, this will not work. How about you stand?" The woman pointed to Brent. "Put one knee up on the crate and wrap the rope about your shoulder."

Brent followed her directions and after a few adjustments, struck a pose the photographer loved.

"Now you lean against his leg and hold the gun across your lap." She motioned the position she wanted to Sam. "But be sure and look at your man."

Brent's face heated. "We're not a couple."

"You are today." The photographer motioned for him to stare down at Sam. "Hmm, can you put your hand on her shoulder?"

Brent dropped his right hand to rest on Sam's shoulder. As it landed, a spark ran up his arm.

"Perfect, now hold that pose."

The lights flashed, and Brent heard the clicking of the camera, but he couldn't remove his eyes from Sam. He should not be developing feelings for this woman he'd probably never see again, but he couldn't convince his heart of that.

"Okay, now a silly pose. Why don't you wrap the rope around her as if you've lassoed her?"

With a smile, Brent helped Sam stand and circled the rope about her waist. The sweet smell of strawberries flooded his nose again as he leaned close to her. Her breath caught, and he found her eyes. Desire and fear fought for control in the deep blue depths. His lips parted, but before he could move, the camera flashed.

"That was perfect. You can come see them this afternoon."

Brent didn't want the shoot to end. He wanted another minute with Sam this close to him. He wanted to know what would happen if he touched her lips, but the moment was gone.

She leaned away from him and untangled herself from the rope before replacing her gun on the prop table. Following her lead, he coiled the rope and added it.

After clearing his throat, he glanced at his watch. "Almost time, shall we go hear the rules?"

"Let's do it."

The crowd had grown while they were busy, and without thinking, Brent grabbed her hand as they edged their way forward. A warm tingling raced up his arm at her touch, and he dared a glance at her.

She returned his gaze, a mixture of emotions on her

face. His eyes dropped to her lips, but before anything further could happen, the crackle of a megaphone interrupted the moment.

Blake, the man from the welcome table, stood on a picnic bench, megaphone in hand. "Welcome everyone to the Cowboy shootout. Cara will hand out the paint guns. Every person gets one. You'll also get a colored badge. Blues are one team. Reds are the other. You can use the space from the post office to the general store. If you get tagged in the chest or the head, you must exit the game. The last person standing will be deemed the winner. Questions?"

A murmuring ran through the crowd, but no one braved a question. Brent pulled Sam over to the table where Cara was handing out guns and badges.

"Hello again. Same team or different?"

"Same," the two answered together, and a feeling he hadn't experienced in years flickered in his heart.

She handed them each a blue badge, a gun, and an ammo packet. Forced to drop Sam's hand, he gathered the supplies, but he missed the warmth.

"That's all you have, so shoot wisely. Have fun you two." She winked at them before turning to the next couple.

Brent checked out the gun which resembled a six shooter though the barrel was much longer and a black air pressure container stuck out from the bottom of the handle. The cylinder didn't open, but a hole in the front allowed the balls to be inserted and then the cylinder turned to engage them. He loaded five pellets into the chamber - as much as it would allow. It would be slow, but he had enough ammo for three reloads. After slipping the gun into the holster around his waist, he dropped the extra ammo in a pocket on the other side and looked up, expecting to need to help Sam, but she had already filled hers as well and was placing the gun in her holster.

"You've shot before."

"Yeah, my dad taught me before I went to college. He wanted to make sure I could protect myself."

"Somehow, I doubt you'd have any issue taking care of yourself."

With a step, Brent closed the distance between them, but as he reached for her hand, the megaphone crackled again.

"Pick your starting places," Connor's voice blared.

Around them, people raced to secure their positions. Sam grabbed his hand this time and pulled him back toward the post office. Warmth traveled up his arm. Several others joined them, and at noon a gun fired into the air. Around them, people rushed out into the open, but Sam and Brent took a slower pace, running from one building to the next place of safety. Brent kept his eyes peeled for red badges.

The sound of pops and groans from hit people filled the air. Brent snagged a few people with red badges before taking a shot to the arm. That didn't disqualify him, but it stung a little. Beside him, Sam rubbed her calf where she had taken a shot.

The image distracted him long enough he didn't see the teen with the red badge until it was too late. Red paint spread on Sam's chest, and she fell to the ground, surprised by the impact.

"No," Brent yelled as he rushed over to her. When the pellet hit his back signaling he was out, he didn't even care.

"You sacrificed yourself for me," Sam joked up at him, clutching her chest and batting her eyes. She played the trope part of a dying lover well.

"I had to." He brushed her hair back from her forehead. He meant it to be funny, but a blanket of emotion covered his shoulders as he stared down at her. The urge to kiss her pulsed through his veins, but he swallowed it. He wasn't sure she was open to it, and he didn't want to overstep any bounds. "I need someone to fix my car."

Sam snickered and swatted his hand away. "Ever the gentleman."

He smiled, covering up the warring emotions battling in his brain. If she only knew.

# CHAPTER 6

S am dusted off her backside as she stood. "Since we're out, should we return this gear?"

He shook his head, not ready to part with the Old West clothing. "Let's see if we can keep it a little longer."

The boyish eagerness in his voice elicited a grin and a chuckle from Sam. "Okay, well then what next?"

Brent pulled out the folded map from his pocket and glanced over the options. "It's too early for lunch, so bobbing for apples?"

She pulled back her shoulders and puffed out her chest. "I should tell you I'm a phenom at bobbing for apples, but if you don't mind being schooled, then lead the way."

"Oh, you are, are you?"

His voice contained a teasing tone and his eyes sparkled as he looked at her. The handsome lines of his face stirred a desire within her, and she averted her eyes as the heat between them coursed through her.

Brent cleared his throat and touched the map. "Looks like it's to the market we go then." After folding it, he held out his hand.

Sam took it after a moment's hesitation. Not that she didn't want to hold his hand, but she wasn't prepared for the emotions that were battling in her head and heart.

The two wound their way through the crowd still watching the shootout to the supermarket. Jaxon, a teen employee, and Gabriella, the supervisor of the market, stood at the apple bobbing station. Gabriella's long dark hair was pulled back in a ponytail, and her darker skin glistened in the sun. Sam had been jealous of her beautiful skin tone from the moment she met her.

"Oh, man, are you Derek McCloud?" Jaxon asked as they approached.

"Derek McCloud?" Sam asked.

"My Night Ranger character's name," Brent returned.

"Oh Mylanta," Gabriella sighed. "I've seen every one of your movies. Do you think we could get an autograph?"

"Sure, do you have a pen?" Brent patted his chaps. "I didn't really bring one with me."

Jaxon pulled one out of his pocket while Gabrielle looked around for something to write on, but there was nothing close.

"Would you sign our shirts?" she asked.

Brent chuckled. "Sure, it wouldn't be the first time."

"It's Gabriella, and this is Jaxon with an x."

"Man, I gotta tweet about this too." Jaxon whipped out his phone and snapped a picture as Brent signed Gabriella's shirt.

"Here, let's take one together." Brent wrapped his arm around Jaxon and smiled as Jaxon snapped another picture. Then he signed Jaxon's shirt as well.

"Thanks Mr. McCloud."

"You can call me Brent, and you're welcome."

"Are you two ready then?" Gabriella asked, but her eyes never left Brent's face.

"Sure, Gabriella. I told Brent here about my bobbing skills, so how do we get started?"

"There are twelve apples in each bucket. You can bob from this one and Brent can bob from Jaxon's. We'll start the timer. You have one minute and whoever gets the most wins."

Sam tucked her hair behind her ears and turned to Brent. "You ready?"

He smiled at her challenge and took up a position in front of Jaxon's bucket, folding his arms behind his back.

Sam assumed a similar stance and waited for the cue to begin. When she heard the bell, she dipped her head into the water. The warm water held no shock, but the apples were large and kept slipping away. She sank her teeth into one, pulled it out and dropped it in the collection bucket. Water dripped into her eyes as she returned for more.

"Time," Gabriella said a moment later.

Sam wiped her eyes, disappointed in the haul. She had lost her touch.

"Sam has five apples." Gabriella counted her stack and then turned to Brent's larger stack, "and Brent has ... ten? Wow, impressive work for one minute. You must be a man of many talents."

A mischievous smile flitted across Brent's face, and he shrugged. "What can I say? I'm a natural."

"You get to pick a prize from the top shelf." Gabriella pointed to a silver rack against the storefront housing stuffed animals and other prizes. "Thanks for playing and thanks again for the autograph. Have fun you two." After shooting Sam a conspiratorial wink, Gabriella turned to the next contestant.

"You played me." Sam pointed her finger at him as they moved over to the shelf.

"You're the one who bragged you were a phenom. You never asked me if I was any good. I simply let you think you'd win. Now pick." Brent motioned to the top shelf.

"No, you won, so you get to pick."

"But I want it to be something you'll enjoy as I'm giving it to you. Consider it a thank you for letting me crash at your place." Brent's eyes held her gaze, and more than a thank you flickered in them.

Sam turned her head and pointed to a stuffed bear on the top wearing cowboy boots and a cowboy hat. Brent stretched up, plucked it off the shelf, and handed it to her.

As their fingertips touched, another spark ran up her arms, and she flicked her eyes up to see him staring down at her.

Her heart thudded so loudly in her chest she feared it was audible. His eyes danced back and forth as they looked from her eyes to her mouth and back. It was obvious Brent wanted to kiss her, but he was leaving Monday. There was no point in allowing an experience if he would be gone in less than forty-eight hours.

"Lunch?" Sam took a step back severing the connection. Brent stared at her a moment longer before nodding and following her to the café.

"So, have you really signed people's shirts before?" Sam asked as she and Brent sat at one of the free tables.

"You would be surprised what I've signed," Brent said with a laugh.

"Oh, my goodness, are you Derek McCloud?" the blonde waitress asked as she approached the table. Sam recognized her from church, but didn't know her well.

"Does this happen everywhere you go?" She asked as Brent signed a napkin for the waitress.

"Not everywhere. Some people are like you and haven't seen my movies."

"But don't you get tired of it all?"

Brent's smile faded and his voice turned serious. "Yeah, sometimes I do."

Silence fell then and Sam bit the inside of her lip. She hadn't meant to ruin the mood.

The waitress returned a moment later and took their order, but the silence remained.

"Do you ever think about giving it up?" Sam finally asked.

Brent looked at her. "I started writing a story last night. It may not amount to much, but it felt good to be writing again. I'd forgotten how much I missed it. And yes, I often think about giving it up." He paused for a moment. "Do you ever think about living somewhere bigger?"

Sam shook her head. "I don't know. I lived in the city once, and it wasn't quite what I hoped it would be. Small town life just suits me better I guess."

The food arrived and, after a prayer, they both dug in, but Sam couldn't help wondering if Brent was thinking as she was - that they were just too different to make something work.

After lunch, they climbed up on the wagon for a hay ride, but although forced to squeeze next to each other, Brent did not take her hand again. Sam fought the urge to grab his, knowing it would only send a conflicting message. She had sent off a signal she wasn't ready for more. Now, she needed to convince her heart of that.

After the ride, they returned the rented gear and stopped into City Hall to pick up their picture before calling it a day.

"Ah, you've returned. Which pose do you prefer?" the woman asked as she laid out two pictures.

Sam's eyes fixed on the silly pose. The photographer

had captured the emotion flowing between them. No one had stared at her like that in ages.

The photographer caught her eye. "That's my favorite too. You two make the cutest couple."

"That one it is then." Brent pulled money out of his pocket.

"Wait, we only get one picture?" Sam asked. "But who will keep it?"

"I suppose you must share it." The photographer winked at the two of them.

Sam didn't miss the subtle hints, but come Monday, Brent would leave, and this time would be nothing more than a memory. Her heart ached at the realization.

Brent took the picture, and they turned to exit, almost running into Skylar and Jasmine, who worked at the diner. As Sam watched Jasmine snuggle into Skylar's arm, a pang of jealousy stabbed her heart. If only Brent weren't returning to Houston. If only they weren't from different worlds.

After clearing her throat, she pasted on a smile and looked up at him. "Ready?"

He motioned for her to lead the way, and they trekked back to the truck. The late afternoon sun cast shadows on the pavement, and Sam's mind wandered. What would kissing Brent McKasson be like?

She sneaked a glance at Brent as she opened the door. He looked as exhausted as she felt, but happy. The stiff city posture was gone from his shoulders, and his face had relaxed into a natural smile instead of the tight scowl he had worn when she first met him.

Sam's cheeks warmed as she imagined his strong arms around her. Brent's brown hair rustled in the breeze, and she couldn't help picturing running her fingers through it or imagining his face pressed against hers.

*Get ahold of yourself, Sam. You said you would not fall for this guy.*

She blinked to clear the image and climbed in the truck, but the thought stayed. He had seemed so different, donning cowboy gear and even losing the shootout to check on her. Then there had been the almost kisses. Why hadn't she let the kiss happen? She needed to know if this connection between them was real.

Sam glanced down at the stuffed cowboy bear resting on the seat in between them. Today had been the most fun she'd had since moving here though that was mainly her fault.

Having not developed a close friendship in town yet, she had thrown herself into work. She'd dined at Marnie's a few times and even ventured into the Silver Spoon once on karaoke night, but everyone had seemed so close that she wasn't sure she would fit in, so she'd never really tried. Once she'd met Fanny and Norma and the others who lived on the outskirts of town, she had stayed closer to home more often, but most of them were much older and had other interests. Her loneliness had been buried until

Brent showed up and reminded her how to have fun again.

Now, the issue was that he wouldn't be staying. His part would be in Monday, and unless it was more than his AOS, she could fix his car and have him on the road by midafternoon at the latest.

"That was fun today." His words broke the silence and he turned to look at her.

"Yeah, it was. I'm glad we went, though I think I will have a few nasty bruises." The shot to the chest had knocked the wind out of her when it hit, but the one she had taken to the leg smarted more. Sam hadn't felt pain like that since she tried martial arts in college and took a kick to the shin that had ached for weeks.

"Yeah, my day job isn't usually so dangerous." The smile he flashed sent a fluttery sensation down her spine. "I have a stunt double for all those scenes."

"What did you write last night? If it's okay to ask."

Brent pinched his lips together and ran a hand over his chin. "I don't know. Last night, a story came to me about a man giving his all to God after tragedy. I have no idea where it's going or if I'll even publish it, but your words inspired the idea."

A slow burn crept up Sam's neck to the top of her ears. "Well, if you're looking for more inspiration, you could join me tomorrow for church. Pastor Ron is a good speaker."

"I'd like that."

When they arrived at the house, Brent excused himself to the spare room to write more and Sam curled up on the couch with her Bible. She read through her devotional, but she couldn't keep her mind off Brent and how her life would be empty again come Tuesday.

# CHAPTER 7

*B*rent threw on his nicest shirt, wishing his bag contained something a little dressier for church. Of course, he hadn't planned on attending church this trip, but he hadn't planned on meeting a girl like Sam either.

It was too bad confusion overshadowed the enjoyable activities of the previous day. The strong urge to kiss Sam had plagued him the entire day, but every time the opportunity arose, she pulled away. Was she hung up on him being from the city? Was it his money? Or did the fact he'd be leaving tomorrow play more of a role? Long distance relationships proved challenging, but Sam was special. Brent would try dating if she'd be open to it, but he wasn't sure of her feelings.

When they had returned to her place, he had locked himself in his room, determined to write through the confusion. Words had appeared, but the confusion hadn't left. The story was coming along well though, and if nothing else, he was thankful for the inspiration.

"You look nice." Sam handed Brent a mug of coffee as he entered the kitchen. "Two sugars. That's the way you drink it, right?"

His heart tightened at the familiar gesture. Sam knew his preferences already, and he could picture similar breakfasts in the future, but perhaps this was merely hospitality. Brent wished, for the first time in years, he found women easier to read. "Thank you."

"So, I wanted to talk about yesterday." Sam sat at the table, her eyes focused on the mug in her hands as if it was a lifeline.

"I enjoyed the time with you." Brent sat across from her, wondering what else was coming.

"I did too." She paused for a moment, twirling the mug in circles. "But I wanted to explain myself. I think you're great, and I had a wonderful time."

His smile faltered at her words. He could hear the 'but' coming.

"But you'll be leaving tomorrow, and I don't know if we should start something that probably won't last." She sneaked a glance at him through lowered lids.

There it was. Brent's heart dropped to his feet though he agreed her words made sense. "Yeah, you're probably right. I'll return to Houston soon and I travel a lot for work. And your life is here."

"Exactly." But her words fell flat, and he wondered if she really meant them or if she was trying to convince herself.

"Of course, I could fly out to see you or fly you to wherever I am. I have the money, Sam."

A spark of hope flickered in eyes for a moment before disappearing. "But how long would that last, Brent?"

As long as it needed to was what he wanted to say, but he could see her wall was back up. There would be no convincing her right now.

"Come on." She stood and placed her mug in the sink. "We need to head out to make it to church on time."

During the quiet ride to church, Brent searched for something to say to lighten the mood, but nothing came to mind.

Sam pulled into a parking space, and the two headed into the white church.

"Good morning." An plump older woman with graying hair smiled at them as they walked in the door.

"Good morning, Tina." Sam leaned in to hug the elder woman. "This is my friend Brent McKasson. He's visiting for the weekend. Brent, this is Tina, the pastor's wife."

"Good to meet you, Brent. I hope you enjoy the service."

Brent nodded and grabbed the paper she held out. He glanced at it as he followed Sam into the sanctuary. It was a bulletin, listing the upcoming events and notes for the day's sermon.

Sam chose a seat near the middle and Brent sat beside her. A few people wandered over and introduced themselves, but Brent's mind remained on the woman to his left. Agreeing to be friends was one thing but sitting next to her and smelling her sweet scent presented a whole new issue.

When the pastor spoke, Brent tried to keep focused on the sermon, but images of Sam kept flooding his mind. He wanted to experience her lips against his own.

Before he realized it, the sermon ended. The only thing he could recall was something about God's timing. Was that what he needed to do? Did he need to wait on God's timing? It had been so long since he'd spoken with God that he felt rusty, but when the pastor closed the service with a final prayer, he asked God for clarity and peace.

"Want to get some lunch?" Sam asked, touching his arm.

Brent opened his eyes and nodded. "Sure, sounds good."

"Marnie's is close and they have good food." Sam led the way across the street.

Marnie's was a small casual restaurant, similar to Norma's though a bit larger. A young perky blonde met them as they entered.

"Welcome to Marnie's on Madison. I'm Becky, and I'll be your waitress today. Just the two of you?"

Brent blinked at the sheer speed the words had exited the woman's mouth.

"Yes, just the two of us," Sam said.

"Follow me." The girl turned and led them to a back booth. She placed two menus down and took their drink order before leaving them.

"So, don't get me wrong," Brent began as he looked around the homey interior of the small place, "but does this town have any elegant restaurants? I mean if I wanted to take a date somewhere," he paused, searching for the right word, "classier?"

Sam smiled at him from across the table. "Are you letting your inner snob surface, Brent McKasson?"

"No, it's just that this doesn't have a 'date like' atmosphere. Surely, this town has at least one date night restaurant."

"That would be Ernesto's. It's an upscale Italian place, but other than that, you'd probably have to drive to one of the bigger towns."

Brent filed the information away in case the opportunity arose in the future.

"I'm sorry, I couldn't help overhearing. Are you *the* Brent McKasson, the movie star?" The voice belonged to a pretty redhead in a yellow summer dress.

"I am," Brent said.

The woman's eyes lit up with excitement. "Do you

think I could bother you for an autograph and a picture? I'm a huge fan."

Brent glanced to Sam who shrugged and waved her hand in a 'go ahead' gesture.

"Sure." Brent looked back to the woman. "Do you have something to write with?"

The woman placed a napkin and a pen on the tabletop in front of him. "Can you make it out to Sandy?"

Brent smiled and shook his head slightly. Signing a napkin wasn't a first for him, but he always wondered what people did with them. Did they really keep them? Frame them on the wall? He scribbled the pen across the surface and then pushed it back to her.

"Can you take a picture of us?" Sandy turned to Sam for the first time, the hopeful question dancing in her eyes.

"Sure." Sam took the camera. Brent couldn't tell if the smirk on her face was from amusement or irritation.

Sandy leaned in, a little too close for Brent's comfort, and Sam tapped the phone. "Okay, here you go."

"Thank you." Sandy once again focused her attention solely on Brent.

"You're welcome."

"I don't think I'd enjoy that, the constant interruption." Sam shook her head as Sandy spun and walked away.

"You get used to it," Brent said.

Becky returned then and took their order, and then a silence fell.

"So, have you always wanted to be a mechanic?" Brent asked.

"Yeah, but a small shop like I have now wasn't really my goal. I had a much bigger shop when I lived in Dallas."

"So, why'd you leave it?" Brent asked.

Sam shook her head. "That's a long story. Let's just say there was a guy involved."

Brent was curious for more information, but it was obvious from Sam's demeanor that the subject was closed. For now at least.

After lunch, they returned to Sam's place. Though he wanted to take her in his arms, he retired to the spare room to work more on his story. He feared too much time around her would make him unable to honor her request to remain just friends.

# CHAPTER 8

Sam stared at the closed door wondering if she should knock. Brent had disappeared to the spare room after lunch to write, but that had been hours ago. After spending time shopping for food and straightening the house, Sam now yearned to see him again. Though he'd be leaving tomorrow, and the desire made no sense, she wanted to spend as much time with him as possible.

The door swung open before her hand could hit the wood.

"Hi, I was coming to see you," Brent began, surprise coloring his voice.

"Would you like to watch a movie?" Sam asked simultaneously.

The two paused and laughed, easing some of the

tension that hung in the air. Brent broke the silence first. "I would love to. I've hit a wall with my writing, anyway."

"Oh, sorry. Are you sure you don't need to keep going?"

Brent's eyes twinkled, the dimple appearing in his cheek. Oh, how she longed to touch that cheek, to experience the texture.

"No, I'm good as long as we don't watch one of my movies. Come on." He grabbed her hand, leading the way to the living room. Sam's lips curled into a small smile. Though it was her house, she liked the fact he took control.

After surfing the channels for a moment, Brent landed on a movie they could agree on—a romantic comedy from a few years ago. Though the movie was interesting, the distance between them fixated Sam's attention. Should she scoot closer? She had been the one to push the friend issue, but the masculinity emanating from him was changing her mind. Brent's strong arms held the appeal of safety, and the woodsy aroma he exuded sent her heart racing.

With a sideways glance her direction, he shifted position, placing his right arm on the back of the couch as if inviting her to move in. Her racing heart overruled her brain's objection, and she closed the space between them. Though his lips curled into a knowing smile, his gaze remained on the television.

Brent's chest was strong, masculine, and Sam's vivid imagination flashed images of her hands splayed across it before her eyes. When his arm moved from the back of the couch to her shoulder, she did not object, but enjoyed the warmth and security provided.

When the movie ended, his face turned to hers. Desire flooded his eyes, and Sam's breath caught. Brent's left hand brushed a loose tendril behind her ear sending a tremor down her spine. Sam's lips parted of their own accord, and his eyebrow twitched as if asking permission to kiss her. She should say no, but her body seemed frozen in place, watching the moment in slow motion.

When his eyes closed as his face lowered, the trance shattered. With the last ounce of resistance, she pushed against his chest. "Brent, we can't. I'm sorry."

With a sigh, his opened his eyes and nodded. "You're right. I should get back to work, anyway."

As his arm dropped from her shoulders, Sam missed the warmth, and a part of her wanted to reach out, to tell him she changed her mind, but it was better this way. As she watched him walk away though she wondered if that were true.

～

*W*hen the alarm blared the next morning, Sam fought the urge to throw it across the room. Brent had worked the rest of the evening in the spare room, not even emerging for dinner, and she had lain awake half the night rehashing the afternoon.

After rubbing eyelids that seemed glued together, she managed a few blinks before struggling out of bed and into the shower.

The warm water proved invigorating, and by the time she was dried off and dressed, she felt almost human. The aroma of coffee woke her further as she padded into the kitchen.

"So, the part should be in today, huh?" Brent looked up from his coffee mug and caught her eyes.

Did she detect a hint of sadness in his voice? Was it possible he didn't want to leave even with her pushing him away? She walked past him to the cupboard.

"Yes, the delivery email stated ten a.m. I figure it will take a few hours to get the new part installed and check it." Sam kept her back turned to him as she spoke, afraid her emotion would show through. Though she'd insisted on only wanting to be friends, she hadn't meant it. It was a defense mechanism to keep from getting hurt again.

"Oh."

That one word carried so much emotion. After filling a coffee mug, she joined him at the table and glanced his direction. His gaze locked with hers. Brent turned his mug around in circles, fingers tapping against the side with each spin. "Thank you for a great weekend. For the festival on Saturday and church and the movie yesterday."

"You're welcome."

The stare lasted a moment longer before he dropped his gaze. "You didn't like me when we first met." His eyes flicked back up. "Why?"

If he had asked on the first day, she would have told him it was none of his business, but over the last few days, he had opened up to her. It was time she did the same and shared her story.

"You remember the man I mentioned at lunch yesterday?"

Brent nodded.

Sam took a deep breath before allowing her mind to wander down memory lane. "I met Greg as I was finishing trade school in Irving. He lived in Dallas, and he helped me find a local shop that was going out of business. I took out a loan and opened up shop. Business was slow at first, but then it grew steady. The hours were long the first few months, but Greg was successful, wealthy, and driven. He claimed he didn't mind.

"I thought we were happy, but one night he cancelled dinner saying he had to work late. I had already closed up shop, so I decided to ride my motorcycle through town as it was a nice night. I saw him holding hands with his secretary. Evidently, he had been seeing her for months. When I confronted him about it, he told me that I was still too country, that city life didn't look good on me.

"Two days later, my mom was killed. I took her death and the breakup as a sign to get my life right with God.

Church hadn't been a priority when Greg was in the picture. My dad took off to go find himself after Mom's death, so going home wasn't an option, and my brother was still serving overseas." She shrugged, "I closed my eyes and pointed to a spot on the map, and I ended up here."

Sam lifted the mug, taking a sip of the coffee before continuing. "When I met you, you reminded me of Greg. Rich and flighty with women."

"You're a good judge of people." Brent stated the words simply and matter-of-factly.

She glanced up, surprised he would admit it.

"I was exactly that," he continued. "I don't even remember the names of some women I've dated recently, but I wasn't always like that." Brent's face tilted up as if recalling a memory. "I was married once to a wonderful woman, Rachel. She was a believer, like you, but a traditionalist. She wanted to stay home and raise kids. We never had any though because she was killed by a drunk driver coming home from the grocery store one day."

Sam's grip tightened on the mug. "Brent, I'm so sorry."

A small, tight smile played across his lips. "Me too. There isn't a day I don't miss her, but I'm glad I met you. You helped me work through some anger I was holding onto about her death, and you helped me find hope again. You even made me realize that women are all different and talented in many areas. I'm sorry for misjudging you and for thinking you couldn't fix my Porsche. I mean you even inspired me to write a story. I'm glad my car broke down here."

As his eyes locked with hers, emotions flooded through Sam. She wanted to ask him to stay, but her pride wouldn't let her. Why had she expressed she only wanted to be friends? She didn't want to be friends, at least not *just* friends. She wanted to tell him of her attraction, but what would be the point with him leaving later? Sam pushed the image of the two of them together from her mind, scooted her chair back, and stood, taking the coward's way out.

"Speaking of your car, I should head to the shop to wait for that part."

"Sam, wait."

His hand stayed her arm as she passed. Heat swept up her skin at his touch, but before he could say anything, she shook her head. "You're leaving, Brent. Let's not."

His eyes searched hers, asking if that was what she really wanted. With a nod, he released her arm and Sam continued out of the house, not looking back.

She held it together until she got in her truck, but as the door closed and the silence set in, the tears trickled down her cheeks. She wasn't sure she was in love with him, but he had shone a spotlight on the loneliness in her life, and she enjoyed having him around. Returning to life the way it was before Brent McKasson showed up now held little appeal.

The drive to her shop was short, and after putting the vehicle in park, she ran a hand across her cheeks to clear away the wet tracks. She had work to finish and no time for the emotions roiling inside her.

# CHAPTER 9

*B*rent stared at the door long after Sam shut it. She kept insisting she wanted nothing more than friendship, but her actions expressed a different story. However, his mother had instructed him to value a woman's requests, and so he would leave, though every bone in his body wanted to stick around.

Not desiring to leave a mess, Brent washed out the mugs from breakfast and set them in the drying rack. As he turned to examine the rest of the kitchen, he wondered if Sam would revert to her previous ways. A week from now, would the odor of spoiled food permeate the air? Would her fridge include only condiments again?

As he thought back to Friday, the front porch steps flashed into his mind. Though no carpenter, he had taken shop in high school and had promised himself he would fix them before leaving, but time had gotten away from him. If he didn't do it now, he might never get the chance, and they wouldn't last much longer. The idea of Sam falling through and breaking an ankle or worse spurred him into action.

In the garage, he found what he needed—a hammer, nails, and a few pieces of wood. It wouldn't be the total fix he would like to do, but it would reinforce the steps and make them safe to walk on.

The morning air still held a chill and the sun's heat wasn't overwhelming, which he was thankful for as attempting the job any later in the day would have been a nightmare. He set the supplies on the ground and then picked up the first sheet of wood. It fit neatly over the bottom step and he smiled as he picked up the hammer and a nail and pounded it into one corner. There was something to the rhythmic pounding that he found relaxing, and his smile grew as he picked up the second nail.

An hour later, he stepped back to admire his handiwork. He had pried off the sagging wood of the two middle steps and replaced them with the wood from her garage. The color didn't match, but she could always paint it if it bothered her. At least this way he would rest easy knowing the steps were safer.

He wiped the sweat from his brow and checked his watch. There was still time to clean up before he figured Sam would call, so he carried the hammer, nails, and rotted wood back to her garage and re-entered the house.

He took a quick shower and had just gotten dressed when his phone rang. "Hello?"

"Brent? It's Sam."

He sank to the bed as she continued speaking. Was it too much to hope the issue was his engine?

"Your car is fixed. Lucky for you it was the AOS, so I can swing by and pick you up in a few minutes if you're ready."

Lucky. He didn't feel lucky. His heart seemed weighted down. "Yeah, I'm ready whenever."

"Okay, I'll be right there."

Brent stared at the now silent phone. He should feel glad that he could continue to the cabin and relax in peace, but his feet drug as he packed up the last of his belongings. Would he be able to write without Sam's presence? A sneaking suspicion she was his muse had wormed its way into his head.

As his fingers touched the photo of the two of them at the festival, he marveled at his emotions after knowing her only a few days. Then again, he'd only known Rachel for a week when he realized he wanted to marry her. Marriage wasn't on his mind right now, but parting with Sam left a bitter taste in his mouth.

After packing the last item in his bag and zipping it closed, he spared one final look around the room, making sure he had missed nothing. Satisfied he had everything from the bedroom, he moved to the kitchen, scanning the rest of the house on his way. Her decorating was not his style at all, but he would miss having someone to drink coffee with in the morning. He'd forgotten that simple joy.

The sound of the horn shattered his daydream, and with a sigh, he hoisted his bags and opened the door to join Sam. It would be a short ride back to her shop, to his car, to the freedom he didn't seem to want any more.

Sam's smile was tight, almost forced as he climbed in the truck. Was she battling the same emotions he was? He perceived, after her story that morning, she'd never want to live in the city again, but could he move? Or could a long-distance relationship work?

Moments later the shop came into view, and Sam parked the truck. With feet that felt encased in concrete, he followed her inside.

As she stepped behind the counter, she cleared her throat. "So, the bill shows the cost for the part and the labor." The paper slid across the surface, but her eyes flickered to his only briefly.

Payment. How had that escaped his mind? No wonder she appeared so uncomfortable. He picked up the bill, pulled out his platinum VISA, placed the card on the bill, and pushed it back her way.

In silence, she rang up the sale and pushed his card back. Then, from her pocket, she pulled out his keys and handed them over.

He took them, wishing he had more to say; wishing he understood what he wanted, what she wanted. "Perhaps

I'll stop by on my way back through." The words sounded hollow and trite to his ears.

"I'd like that."

With a final, awkward handshake, he exited the shop and climbed in the Porsche. The leather still molded to his body, but something seemed different. Stella was different. No, not Stella, *he* was different.

The engine started without a hitch and no smoke billowed out from under the hood. With a sigh, he put the car in gear and pulled out onto Willow Street. After passing the market where he bought food for their first dinner together, he turned right on State. The elementary school appeared on his left, and before he realized it, he was passing the park and leaving Soda Spurs.

Sad country music crooned through the radio, and he flicked the station changer until he landed on an uplifting Christian song. A smile surfaced at the memory of standing next to Sam in church the day before. She had a voice like an angel though she denied it when he told her. Plus, she looked peaceful as she worshipped, eyes closed and hands raised. He wasn't even sure she comprehended doing it half the time. He'd have to find a church and get connected when he returned home. Of course, he wouldn't have Sam standing beside him, and there would be no smell of strawberries and no angelic voice, which saddened him.

An hour later, he pulled up to the cabin, nestled

among a small grove of trees. He parked the car and grabbed his bags.

Julia had given him the key to her family's cabin, promising it would be quiet, and he'd be able to unwind and maybe write, but now it appeared too quiet. He wondered if he'd be able to find his inspiration here like he could at Sam's place.

The second step creaked as he mounted the porch, reminding him of Sam's rickety steps. Had she noticed he fixed them yet? With a shake of his head to dispel the image, he flicked through the keys on the ring for the one to the cabin.

The quaint main room held only a couch, a chair, a table, and a fireplace. Stairs at the back led up to the second story which Julia said housed two small bedrooms and a bathroom. However, since a master bedroom existed downstairs, he didn't expect he'd need to use the upper level.

After setting his bag down in the overstuffed brown chair, he toured the rest of the house. The kitchen was smaller than Sam's, but neat. A dining table sat in the corner. Down the hallway lay the master bedroom with a bath. A king-sized bed topped with a blue and white quilt and a large dresser filled the room. The bathroom matched the minimalist décor of the bedroom.

As he wandered back to the living room, the quiet set in. An old clock above the fireplace ticked away the seconds. With a sigh, he pulled his laptop out of the bag, placed the bag on the floor, and plopped down on the chair. There was no desk here, like at Sam's, and the coffee table was lower than the chair, so his lap would have to suffice.

He read back over the words he had typed out the last few days and found himself lost in the story, but as he reached the end and placed his fingers on the keys, nothing came. No spark, no story, no ideas. Just Sam. Beautiful, challenging, engaging Sam.

She was probably still at the shop as it was not quite four. Did she have a customer or was she sitting and watching the clock hands slowly make their way around the face?

A knock at the cabin door interrupted his daydreaming, and his heart fluttered. Could it be Sam? Had she followed him out here? A smile tugged at his mouth as he opened the door, but it froze quickly. The woman in front of him was *not* Sam.

# CHAPTER 10

*S*am watched the Porsche fade into the distance before re-entering her shop. She still needed to finish the repairs for Rose, even though Rose had insisted there was no hurry, but now that Brent's car was fixed, she had no reason not to work on it. Plus, she needed the money. Brent's repairs would get her through another month, but she needed to get more customers coming in, and word of mouth was the best way to make that happen. Since Rose was a bit of a gossip and ran the only flower shop in town, it might mean a spike in business.

The bell above her door jingled and she glanced up. Had Brent decided to stay after all?

"Excuse me, are you Sam Jenkins?" A man she didn't recognize, dressed nicer than most folks in Soda Spurs stood in her doorway.

"Yes, I'm Sam. What can I do for you?"

The man smiled and waved to someone unseen. Before Sam could react, two more people flooded her shop, one holding a camera and the other a microphone which was shoved unceremoniously in her face.

"I'm Gary with the Star Gazette. We heard Brent McKasson was staying here with you. Are you two an item?"

"What? No!" Sam shook her head and tried to hide her face. "He was just here getting his car fixed, and he's gone now, so you can leave too."

"Is he coming back? Did he tell you about his next movie?" The man continued firing questions as Sam pushed them out of her shop and locked the door.

She leaned against it and shook her head. Maybe it was a good thing Brent had left after all. If this reporter knew he had been here, it probably meant more were on their way, and Sam had no desire to be in the spotlight.

With a sigh, she pushed away from the door and popped the hood of Rose's car to begin her inspection.

When she finished, a glance at the clock showed closing time. At least she'd have the house back to herself. Not that Brent had been a bad roommate, but it was her space, and now it would be quiet and the way she liked it again.

She opened the door quietly and poked her head out first, but no reporters were in sight. Still, she wasted no time locking the shop and racing to her truck.

As she pulled into the driveway, she noticed her steps

no longer appeared the same color. *What happened here?* She stepped out of the truck, looked closer, and realized the wood was different.

She could have replaced them herself; however, with starting her new business, all other aspects of her life had been shoved to the back burner. Moisture pooled in her eyes at the thoughtfulness of Brent, and she sniffed the tears back as she tested the steps. No more sagging, no more squeaking.

After inserting the key in her front door, she told herself one more time how much she'd enjoy the quiet, but as she opened the door and the silence answered her, she doubted the truth of the statement. Sam dropped her keys on the side table and wandered into the kitchen. Not a dish was out of place.

His presence still lingered, a hint of his cologne. If she closed her eyes, she could almost smell the woodsy scent. Hoping the odor would be stronger in the spare room, she meandered down the hallway and opened the door.

The room appeared pristine. The made bed held no wrinkles; no trash littered the room; and the bear he had won her sat prominently on the pillow, a white slip of paper peeking out from underneath. She unfolded the paper as she sat on the bed.

*Dear Sam,*

*Thank you for opening your home. You helped me find my muse. I hope our paths will cross again, and if this story ever amounts to anything, I'll send you a copy. Maybe you'll find time to read this one.*

*-Brent McKasson*

She smiled, remembering the conversation about her mother's books. Sam placed the note down and grabbed the pillow, holding it to her face. His scent was stronger here, but by this time tomorrow, it would be gone and all she'd have left of Brent McKasson was a note and a silly stuffed bear.

What was wrong with her? She had no time for men, especially not rich actors who lived in the city and were constantly hounded by photographers and autograph seekers. She stood, dropping the pillow. A walk; that was what she needed. A walk would clear her mind, get it out of the clouds and back where it belonged.

After locking her door, she headed down the farm market road with no particular destination in mind. However, she was not surprised when she found herself in front of Fanny's porch.

"I figured you'd be by to visit me." Fanny didn't bother looking up from her knitting.

Sam smirked softly as she leaned against the railing, wondering how this woman perceived so much. "Was your room really taken?"

The needles paused, and Fanny pinched her lips together. "Sometimes we need to be uncomfortable to realize God's will for us."

"God's will?" Sam couldn't help but sound skeptical.

"Brent left today, Fanny. So, if you're thinking God's will was for us to be together, that's not happening."

The needles resumed their rhythmic clacking. "Things aren't always what they seem. God has a plan and a purpose, even when we don't understand it at first."

"Well, the only purpose I can see is that it showed me I miss companionship."

The elderly woman didn't answer, just kept clicking her needles.

"All right Fanny, have a nice night."

Fanny paused long enough to raise one wrinkled hand in a wave before refocusing on her needles.

As Sam headed back toward her house, she passed Norma's, paused, and turned back. She had promised she wouldn't eat out so much, but she was hungry and there would be people inside. It was a start at getting involved.

Norma greeted her with a wave as she stepped inside. Sam returned it and sidled up to the counter to order a burger and fries before claiming an empty booth. Only a handful of other people filled the mostly empty restaurant.

"How you doing, hon?" Norma asked as she slid the food in front of Sam and her ample frame into the seat on the other side of the booth. She folded her hands on the table and turned her eyes on Sam.

Sam offered a crooked, half-smile. "I thought I'd be happy, you know? He was so obnoxious when I first met him, but after the festival on Saturday and church on Sunday, I saw a different side of him." Dropping her eyes, she ran her hand up and down the glass of tea, watching the sheen of condensation disappear under her touch. "I guess I hoped he would want to stay and finish his writing here. Did you know he writes as well as acts?"

Norma shook her head and patted Sam's arm. "Did you ask him to stay?"

Sam let out an unattractive snort. "No, in fact, I told him I only wanted to be friends. Why did I do that Norma?"

"Because you were scared, hon. We've all been there. Now, I only met him once, but he seemed like good people. Perhaps he'll surprise you and come back."

Sam shrugged and grabbed a fry. "Maybe, but I'm not holding my breath. Once he gets back to the city, he'll forget all about this town and me. Greg did, and we lived five minutes from each other."

"You can't compare him to a past relationship, hon. Brent is his own person, with his own issues, but he's not Greg." Norma gave her a small smile and one final pat on the arm before scooting out of the booth and heading back to work.

Sam knew she was right. Brent wasn't Greg, but it didn't really matter. He was gone, and she needed to accept that, forget him, and get on with her life.

# CHAPTER 11

"Tricia, what are you doing here?" The two had only dated for a month, but Brent realized it was two weeks too long when she blew up his phone with texts every morning and every night.

"I came to visit you, silly." Tricia placed a perfectly manicured hand on his chest and smiled, batting eyes laden with eyeshadow and fake lashes. "Julia told me you were here, so I thought I'd come see if I could help."

"Oh, she did, did she?" Brent tried to keep his tone light, but inside he seethed. He had informed Julia he needed alone time. Why would she tell Tricia of all people where to find him?

"Well, not willingly." Tricia's too-full lips pushed into a mischievous pout. "I saw pictures of you at some small-town festival and figured Julia could tell me where you were." Her pout turned into a frown. "I can't believe you didn't take me with you. Anyway, I only stretched the truth a little. I told her there was urgent news you needed to hear."

Brent rolled his eyes. He'd have to perform damage control when he got back as there was no telling what lie Tricia had spun. Since gossip magazines rarely got information right anyway, he didn't need them getting wrong information.

"Aren't you going to invite me in?" Her lips returned to a pout and she tilted her head to the side and batted her eyes.

Had he ever found this woman endearing? Or were her negative traits standing out because of the last few days with Sam. Down to earth Sam who didn't need makeup and got ready in five minutes flat. Sam, who, in three days, had managed to steal his heart. Sam, who claimed she wanted to be friends, but acted otherwise. Why had he left? Better yet, why was he still here?

"You know what? You have to go."

"What?" Her brow furrowed together as she placed hands akimbo on her hips.

"Yes. In fact," — he grabbed his bag, shoving the laptop back inside — "I have to go too. I remembered that I left something back in Soda Spurs."

"What is so important that you'd make me leave after just arriving?" Tricia's demeanor quickly shifted from fun and flirty to angry.

"My heart." Brent flashed a quick smile and locked the

door behind him.

"Your what?" She hollered after him as he passed her, leaving her standing on the porch. "Brent, you're making a big mistake."

Brent ignored her, climbed in the car, and fished out the receipt for Sam's repair work. Though silly, it held the only connection to her besides the picture from the Cowboy shootout tucked in his bag. "I'm coming, Sam," he whispered aloud, "and this time I'm not letting you push me away."

Strapping his seatbelt, he backed out of the drive, waving at Tricia as he left.

When he hit the highway, his foot found the accelerator, and a smile crept across his face. He should never have left. He was inspired and he couldn't remember being as content as he had been this last weekend.

As the scenery passed, he imagined what Sam might be doing. Surely, she had left for the day. Would she be at home reading her Bible? Or would she have returned to her old ways and be eating Norma's non-home-cooked food?

Brent's gaze flicked to the left as a flash of light caught his attention. A car was barreling down the road at full speed. Though his foot slammed the brake, it was not fast enough, and the surprised expression of the other driver was the last image he saw before the car slammed into him and the world went dark.

# CHAPTER 12

*A*fter paying the tab, Sam began the short walk home. The sun sat low on the horizon, and a chill floated on the air. A shiver fluttered down Sam's spine, causing her to wish she had brought a light jacket before setting out. From within her pocket, her cell phone vibrated.

Sam glanced at the number as she pulled the phone out. It wasn't familiar, but perhaps the call was a new customer. She just hoped it wasn't another reporter. Did they even do that? Find cell numbers? She hoped not and bit her lip as she pressed the button.

"This is Sam Jenkins. How can I help you?"

The voice was clinical and professional. "Is this the Sam who owns Sam's Repair in Soda Spurs?"

A foreboding feeling blanketed Sam and her feet halted. "Yes, that's me."

"This is Dr. King from St. Joseph's. We are hoping you can assist us. Brent McKasson was in an accident and we are hoping to locate his next of kin, but yours was the only number found in his possessions."

Icy fear flooded Sam's veins. "Is he," she swallowed, choking the emotion down, "Is he okay?"

"It's too soon to tell."

Sam's eyes closed, recalling their conversations over the last few days. They hadn't spoken much about his personal life, but she thought he had mentioned his agent once in their discussion. Julia, she thought that had been the name he said. "I don't know if he has any family, but he has an agent, Julia something, but I'm not sure where she works. Can I come visit him?"

"Of course, though he's in the ICU. Your visiting times may be limited."

"He's in intensive care?" The words escaped as a whisper from her strangled throat.

"That's all I know for now. Thank you for the information."

The phone clicked. Without another thought, Sam jogged the rest of the way home, peeling off her clothes as she entered to change into a pair of sweats and a t-shirt. She wanted to be comfortable in case she faced a long wait.

Sam opened a backpack and shoved in a blanket, a travel pillow, and her hairbrush, toothbrush, and deodorant. With no idea if Brent had family or if Julia would come, she prepared for a lengthy stay. No way she was letting Brent wake up with no one there or worse with reporters if they caught wind of his accident.

After grabbing her wallet, she slung the bag over her shoulder and hurried out to the truck. When the engine roared to life, her foot pressed the pedal. Thankful that the way to St. Joseph's was a straight shot, she focused on prayers.

"Lord, I don't know why you brought Brent into my life, but please be with him now. Heal him if it is your will and help me to be okay with whatever happens."

There were plenty of open spaces in the parking lot at the hospital, and Sam snagged one close to the main entrance. Before opening the truck door, she closed her eyes and took a deep breath. Though she wanted God's will to be done, a large part of her wanted God to heal him. She didn't know how it would work, but she had been a fool not to tell him how she felt. With a heavy sigh, she exited the truck and forced her feet up the sidewalk to the main door.

The doors emitted a small whooshing sound as they slid open to allow entrance. She stepped into the lobby of the hospital, and the mood shifted. Goosebumps erupted on her skin as she scanned the area for someone in charge.

A solitary nurse sat at the check in desk while a few people waited in the chairs around the lobby.

"Hi, I was wondering if there was any news on Brent McKasson? I'm Sam Jenkins. They called me."

The nurse, a petite blonde with her hair pulled back, looked up from the computer. "Hm, let me check." She tapped on the keyboard. "Mr. McKasson came in after an automobile accident. He's in ICU and visiting hours are over for the night."

Sam forced a small smile though her heart had dropped to the floor. "That's okay. I'll stay if it's allowed. Will you please tell me if there's any update?"

The nurse nodded before turning back to the computer.

Turning to scan the options, Sam spied a small couch near the back of the lobby. It wasn't her bed, but it would be much more comfortable than a chair.

She took the pillow out of the bag and curled up on the small couch, glad she had remembered her jacket before leaving. The cool air sent a shiver down her legs, but she curled up and closed her eyes.

~

Sam stretched and checked the time. It was almost seven a.m. How had she slept so long on the uncomfortable couch? As she lifted her arms, her shoulders screamed their hatred at her, and her neck made an audible creaking noise with each roll of her head.

A commotion at the front desk grabbed her attention as she stood to work out the rest of the kinks.

"What do you mean I can't see him? I'm his agent. It

is imperative I see him at once." A brunette woman with a tight bun stood at the front desk, hands splayed across the top. Her pinstripe suit screamed "designer," and Sam crept a little closer, curious if this was Julia.

"Visiting hours don't start for another hour. You can enter then, but not until." The nurse this morning was a stocky brunette who obviously worked out.

Sam intervened. "I'm sorry, I couldn't help but overhear. Are you here for Brent McKasson?"

The woman crossed her arms and shot a narrowed gaze at Sam. "I am. Who are you?"

"Sam Jenkins." She held out her hand. "I fixed his car and spent the weekend with him."

"Julia Adams." Her hand was soft with an immaculate French manicure topping her fingernails, but her eyes were cold and wary as she looked Sam up and down. "You don't look like his usual type."

Sam's face heated. "Oh, no, not like that." Her hand snaked up to scratch her head. Without her usual shower this morning, her hair felt greasy. "The hotel was booked, so he stayed in my guest room."

"Un-huh, I'm sure. It's none of my business, honey, but you obviously want something, so what can I do for you? Did he forget to pay you? Come on to you?"

Sam blinked at the cavalier questions and shook her head. "No, I... it's not like that at all." She took a deep breath and tried again, "Would you care for a cup of coffee? They won't let us visit for another hour, so I thought perhaps you'd like company while you wait."

Julia shot another glance at the nurse before turning back to Sam with a fake smile plastered on her face. "Sure, that would be nice. It was an early flight."

"Great, let me get my bag." Sam jogged back to the couch and grabbed her bag, shoving the pillow inside.

Julia's eyebrows arched in surprise as she returned. "You spent the night? I thought you said it wasn't like that."

"When they called me last night, I didn't know if he had anyone else coming. I didn't want him to wake up and be all alone. Plus, I had a reporter at my shop yesterday - I live nearby in Soda Spurs - and I didn't want him hounding Brent. I actually have no idea if the reporter left, but better safe than sorry, right?" Sam shut her mouth to stop the rambling. Though there was more to the story, she didn't feel comfortable sharing her feelings with Julia yet.

Julia nodded, but her raised eyebrow showed she clearly didn't believe Sam. Regardless, she followed her to the lobby elevator.

Sam punched the button for floor three, relieved when the doors opened, and the sounds of the cafeteria greeted them. The breakfast rush was in full swing, but the women snagged coffees, muffins, and an open table.

"So, how long have you been Brent's agent?" Sam asked as she unwrapped her muffin.

"Seven years. When I first met him, he was raw and impulsive, but motivated. I think Rachel helped with that. When she died, Brent sort of lost his way. Now, he keeps talking about wanting something different, but the Night Ranger movies sustain his wealth."

As Julia sipped her coffee, the first signs of emotion flickered in her eyes.

"You care for him, don't you?" Sam asked.

"I do. He's grown on me over the years. When I first received the call he'd been in an accident, my heart stopped, and not because he's my best paying client, although that certainly doesn't hurt. Have you heard anything?"

"No more than you, I'm afraid." She picked off a piece of muffin. "Does he have any other family? I hate the thought of no one being here for him."

"He does, but I'm afraid it's not the best relationship. They didn't agree with him going into acting. I'm not sure they'd even come."

"Oh, that's awful." Even though a distance had grown between Sam and her father after her mother's death, she couldn't imagine he wouldn't show up if she were in an accident.

"It is. I guess I'm the closest thing he has to family, and Tricia maybe, if the rumors are true."

"Rumors?" The word squeaked out as an icy cold sensation pulled at Sam's heart.

"Yes, his ex-girlfriend or maybe current girlfriend

again. I can't keep up. Anyway, she came to my office and stated she had urgent news he needed to know right away. Whenever I've seen a woman that adamant, it's usually because she's pregnant. I wonder if she got a hold of him before the accident."

Sam's stomach sank. What was she doing here? Of course he would have a woman back home though she was surprised he never mentioned her. And it sounded like this was a perpetual cycle for him.

"Well, it's almost eight o'clock. Shall we go ask if they'll let us in?" Julia downed the last of her coffee and folded her muffin wrapper into a perfect square.

"You go ahead. I need to get back to work, anyway." Sam grabbed her bag and pushed her chair back.

"Okay," — the puzzlement was evident in Julia's voice — "well, I'll tell him you stopped by then."

"No need. I doubt he'll remember me anyway, but it was nice meeting you." Sam flashed a wave before hurrying out of the room.

*Why God? Why did you bring him into my life?*

She received no answer as she exited the hospital and climbed into the truck. Tears pricked her eyes as she drove the half hour back to Soda Spurs, but she refused to let them fall. To keep her focus off her breaking heart, she ran down the list of work she still needed to do on Rose's car.

## CHAPTER 13

*B*rent groaned as his eyes opened. His left side burned as if on fire; and his throat was scratchy and parched.

"Good morning, how are you feeling?"

His eyes flicked to the right where Julia sat in a chair near the window tapping away on her tablet.

"What are you doing here?" Brent's voice was quiet as the mere act of breathing sent a shooting pain racing across his chest.

"You think I'd stay in Houston with my best client in the hospital?"

"Ugh, did the doctors tell you what happened because I'm pretty sure I broke a rib." He reached over to find bandages wrapped around his chest.

"Do you not remember the accident?" Julia lowered the tablet and leaned forward, concern evident in her eyes.

Brent smirked and tried not to laugh. "Relax, I remember the accident. I was asking if you knew the extent of the injuries."

"Are you worried about the next movie?" Julia asked, raising an eyebrow as she leaned back in her chair.

"That is on my mind, but more importantly, I need to see a girl and tell her I care for her. I was on my way back to Soda Spurs before the accident."

"Brent, you need to get back to Houston. The studio wants an answer on the script."

Brent opened his mouth to speak, but Julia held up her hand, cutting him off. "I know you stated you wanted something different, but the money on this one is worth it. If you want to try something different after it, you can, but you should finish the Night Ranger series. I was going to call you and tell you to come back by Wednesday, but then I got the call about your accident."

"Julia." Brent's words came out forcefully enough that Julia shut her mouth and stared at him. "I'll be happy to go back with you, but not before I tell Sam how I feel about her."

Julia's face fell, and her fingernail tapped against the tablet in an unconscious gesture. "Sam wouldn't happen to be a petite brunette who fixed your car, would she?"

Hope flooded Brent's body, masking the pain for a moment, and his eyes flicked left, hoping to catch a glimpse of Sam. "Yes, that's her. Is she here?"

A grimace crossed Julia's features as her lips mashed

together and her finger stopped tapping and began tracing an imaginary circle on the screen. "We had breakfast together, and she seemed really nice, but when it was finally visiting time, she left in a hurry. Said not to tell you because you probably wouldn't even remember her."

That didn't sound like Sam at all. "What did you say to her?" Brent grunted as he struggled to sit up, but the angry pain seared through his body. With a grimace, he fell back the few inches he had managed.

Julia's bottom lip folded in under her teeth and her eyes slid to the floor. "I may have mentioned Tricia coming to see you and my suspicion that she was pregnant since she was so adamant to see you. Is she?" Julia leaned forward again, eyes wide as if sharing a juicy bit of gossip.

Irritation replaced the hope that moments ago had surged through Brent. "No, she isn't, and I can't believe you told her where to find me. She showed up at the cabin as if we'd never broken up and she thought she could just waltz in and hang out. There was nothing important to tell me; she simply wanted to sit around the cabin and suck up my energy."

Julia's eyes widened, and her hand covered her mouth. "Brent, I am so sorry. I'll help you fix it. I promise."

"If it is fixable." He relaxed against the pillow as defeat took hold. Sam's last boyfriend had cheated on her. Would she really believe he wasn't doing the same thing? He would need a grand gesture to convince her.

"Ah, good, you're awake."

Brent swiveled his head to focus on the unfamiliar male voice. A short man with a receding hairline and a white lab coat stared back at him.

"I'm Dr. King. Tell me, can you remember the accident?"

"Yeah, some guy on his cell phone plowed through his stop sign and hit me. How bad are my injuries?"

"You have a broken rib. That will be painful, but I'm not terribly worried about it. However, you were unconscious when you arrived and you had a concussion which is why we kept you here overnight."

"Well, I'm awake now and other than the pain in my ribs, I feel fine, so when can I get out of here?"

Dr. King blinked and made a tsking sound. "My, my, my, someone's in a hurry. Do you have some place you need to be?"

"Yes." Brent shot daggers Julia's direction. "I need to go convince a girl I'm not about to be a father."

The doctor looked from Julia to Brent and back again before shrugging and holding up his hands in a 'none of my business' gesture. "I can probably sign your release papers today if you can answer a few questions for me."

"Shoot." Brent perked up at the idea of getting out of the hospital and seeing Sam again.

"Full name?"

"Brent Alexander McKasson."

To the left, Julia snorted. "Your initials spell Bam? How did I never know that?"

Brent rolled his eyes and turned his focus back to the doctor.

"Birthday?"

"November fifteenth."

"What day of the week is it?"

"It's Tuesday."

"Alright, you appear to be recovering well. You may have dizziness and a headache for a few days, but I don't see any lasting damage. As for your ribs, take it easy. Do you do heavy lifting for your job?"

"No worries there," Julia piped up, "This is Brent McKasson, movie star. All he needs to do is deliver lines. He has a stunt double for the action scenes."

The doctor shot her a disapproving glare before turning his attention back to Brent. "Acting should be fine, but no weight lifting. And even though it hurts, I want you to move around. If you lie down too long, you could cause an infection. Try to breathe regularly. You've also got some cuts and other bruises, but the rib appears to be the worst of your injuries. I would say you were lucky."

"Thanks doctor."

"Can he fly? I really need to get him back to Houston by Friday," Julia piped up from the chair.

"Yes, he can fly, but don't fill his schedule too full. He does still need rest. I'll go get your release paperwork in order and have you out of here in a few hours."

As Dr. King exited the room, Brent turned to Julia. "I'll fly back with you on one condition. When we get out of here, you are going to follow my orders to the letter. I need to know Sam understands what happened before I can leave town. You got that?"

Julia nodded as she took notes on her tablet. Her lips pulled into a smile as he laid out his thoughts.

❧

"Where are we going?" Julia asked as she climbed into the rental car.

"To the flower shop in Soda Spurs." Brent pulled the seat belt across his chest and slid it into the buckle. "We are going to buy every last flower for Sam, and if that isn't enough, then we'll order in from the nearest town. We're going to fill Norma's diner, as long as she'll let us. Actually, we better stop there first and make sure it's okay."

"Okay, just give me the address." Julia tapped the GPS to bring it to life.

Brent offered a shrug in apology. "I don't know the address. Just type in Soda Spurs and we'll find it. The town isn't very big, and once we get there, I should remember how to get there."

Julia shook her head as she tapped in the letters. "This girl better be worth it, Brent."

"She is." He couldn't contain the smile that spread across his face. "Believe me, she is."

Half an hour later, they pulled into the small parking lot at Norma's. After exiting the car, Brent led the way up the short walk to the front door. He placed his hand on the handle, but paused before pulling it open. "I hope she isn't eating here today."

"Is that a concern?" Julia asked, a hint of disdain in her voice.

"It may not look like much, but trust me, the food is good."

Julia responded with a raised eyebrow, but she followed him inside.

The inside was empty except for Paul, warming the same barstool he had been sitting at last time. Did the man work?

"Hey, Paul, is Norma around?"

"Course I am." Her voice came from the kitchen and a moment later, she appeared in the doorway, wiping her hands on a towel. "I thought Sam said you left town. Wait, what happened to you?" In a few large steps, she halved the distance between them.

Brent's hand touched the cuts on his head. "I did leave, but then I realized I cared for Sam and was on my way back when I was involved in a car accident."

"Then what are you doing here?" Norma asked, crossing her arms. "Does she know you're back?"

"Not yet." Brent shot a pointed look at Julia. "There was a misunderstanding at the hospital, so I have something I need to do first. Could I possibly take over your restaurant tonight for a few hours? I can pay you for any lost wages."

"Honey, it's a Tuesday night. Other than Paul here, there won't be much business anyway. What do you have in mind?"

"I'm going to buy every flower in Rose's shop and fill this place with them. Do you think you could get her here?"

"Sure, I'll just tell her my truck broke down again," Paul spoke up. "Happens about every two weeks anyway, so she won't think nothing of it."

"That's perfect." Norma's eyes danced as she rubbed her hands together. "I'll call Fanny too and let her know to come over."

"I thought you didn't have a phone." Brent suddenly had the feeling he had been played.

Norma laughed and shared a look with Paul. "Of course I have a phone, but I needed to know you were good people first."

Brent shook his head. Only in a small town. "All right, Julia here and I will go get the flowers. Just keep Sam away from here."

"Will do. I guess I better clean up a bit around here."

"Is that the nicest restaurant in town?" Julia asked as they climbed back in her rental car.

Brent held his side as he chuckled. "No, but Norma serves good food and has been a friend to Sam. I'd rather surprise her here."

"I guess." Julia did not sound convinced as she started the car. "Which way now?"

Brent navigated the few streets to the town flower shop. The bell jingled above the door, announcing their entrance as they stepped inside. Rose, a petite redhead, glanced up from the front counter. "Hi, how can I help you?"

"I'm not sure you remember me, Rose, but I was with Sam Jennings this weekend."

Rose's eyes widened in recognition. "Of course, I thought you looked familiar."

"Are these all the flowers you have?" Brent glanced around the store. He wasn't sure if these would even be enough.

"No, there's more in the back in refrigeration." Rose's words were slow and hesitant. "Why?"

"I need all of them. Every flower you have. Arranged and brought over to Norma's by six pm."

"That's only a few hours from now," Rose stammered.

"Then hire some help. Money is no object."

Rose blinked at him. "You're talking thousands of dollars. And that's just in flowers alone."

Brent nodded. "That's fine. I'll leave you my credit card information and you can give the final copy to my agent Julia here. Julia, meet Rose. Rose, Julia." The two women exchanged a small wave.

"Okay, let me see who I can get to come help me,"

Rose said. "It may take me a minute to go through my contacts."

"We'll be here." Brent flashed her a smile as Rose shook her head and picked up the phone.

"Lucky Sam," she mumbled under her breath.

# CHAPTER 14

*S*am sighed as she finished her devotional for the evening. She hadn't been able to keep her mind off Brent. Perhaps she should have stayed at the hospital, to make certain he was okay; however, the prospect of running into a girlfriend held no appeal for her. She had convinced herself that by throwing energy into work, she could forget about him, but she had failed miserably.

Her fingers grasped her cell phone, hovering over the keypad. Surely, it wouldn't hurt to call and make sure he was okay. Brent would never need to know. After another moment of waffling, she took a deep breath and looked up the number for St. Joseph's, punching the call button before her mind changed.

"St. Joseph's hospital, how may I direct your call?" The feminine voice on the other end sounded friendly, which bolstered Sam's courage.

"Hi, I was hoping to get an update on Brent McKasson. He's a friend of mine who was in an automobile accident yesterday."

"Let me check." The sound of clicking keys carried through the phone as Sam held her breath, waiting. "Ah, it appears Mr. McKasson checked out this morning."

Like a stone, Sam's heart thudded to the floor. "Oh, okay, thank you." She ended the call and stared at the screen. He hadn't called her while in the hospital or after being released. She must have imagined his attraction then. *Good thing I didn't stay and make a fool of myself.*

The sudden vibration of the phone caused her to jump and the device tumbled from her hand and landed face up on the carpet. A local number showed on the caller ID, but Sam couldn't place whose number it was.

"Hello?"

"Sam? It's Paul. My truck's broken down at Norma's again. Can you come help?"

"Of course. Be right there." Shoving the phone in her pocket, Sam grabbed a jacket and her keys and headed out to the truck. Paul was beginning to be one of her regular clients. His old Ford seemed to break down every other week at least. She had tried convincing him to replace it, but he insisted the truck still had life in it.

Paul's truck was parked in front of Norma's, but Sam walked past it, wanting to find out what Paul had already tried first. No need to repeat something he had already done. As the front door opened, the overpowering smell of flowers hit her. What was going on here? Norma was not the floral type.

The lights inside the restaurant were dim, but light enough for Sam to see a magnificent rose arrangement on every table and covering the bar. Yellow, red, white, and pink varieties filled every bouquet. What was going on?

"Norma? It's me, Sam."

No voice answered her, and Sam stepped further into the dining area, looking for Norma and Paul.

The kitchen door swung open, and her heart skipped a beat.

Brent stood in the doorway. Dark stubble covered his cheeks and chin and there were a few cuts on his forehead which hadn't been there when he left, but his eyes—those warm pools of chocolate that melted her heart—hadn't changed.

She wanted to rush to him, to tell him how much she missed him, but she refrained, crossing her arms instead. If he was about to spew slick words at her, she wanted her defenses intact. "What are you doing here? And where's your girlfriend?"

Brent turned his head to the side. "Julia?"

Julia's head poked through the doorway over Brent's shoulder. An expression of contrition covered her face, and her lips pursed together. "I may have been mistaken about Tricia. It turns out she isn't pregnant, and they broke up weeks ago and didn't get back together." She threw a glare at Brent. "A fact Brent could have told me sooner and saved everyone some trouble."

Sam took a step back as the emotional wall came crashing down, but there were still questions she needed answers to before she allowed her heart to soar. "Okay, so you don't have a girlfriend who's pregnant. That still doesn't explain what you're doing here."

Brent's lips parted in a full smile, showing off his perfect white teeth. "Must I spell it out for you, Sam Jenkins? I'm here for you." With light footsteps, he crossed from behind the bar to a few feet in front of Sam. "You were all I thought of when I left on Monday, and the cabin seemed too quiet and empty. Then Tricia showed up, making me realize I didn't want quiet or her. I wanted you. When the accident happened, I was on my way back to Soda Spurs to see you."

Her heart pounded in her chest, urging her to step into his arms, but she still had questions. "But why didn't you call me? Why didn't I hear from you?"

With another step forward, he took her hand. Sam enjoyed the warmth that traveled up her arm.

"When Julia filled me in on what happened, I figured you wouldn't believe me unless I could tell you in person, but they wouldn't release me until they were sure I was alright. Evidently, I had a small concussion, but as soon as I was released, I drove here. It was torture not calling you, but it allowed me to plan this." He motioned to the extravagant flowers filling the room.

Joy pulsed through Sam as his fingers entwined with hers. "But what about your career? Won't you be returning to Houston soon?"

"Yes, I do need to return to Houston. In fact, I need to fly back Thursday, but I want to spend the next few days with you."

"And what happens after that?" Sam asked. A few days would be fantastic, but she had a business here. And Brent's life was in Houston. Could they really make it work?

"We'll figure that out." Brent squeezed her hand tighter. "I've got plenty of money. I can drive out or fly you to Houston for weekends until we decide. I don't know what the future holds, Sam, but I'd like you in it. You're kind of my muse." His eyebrows inched up in an endearing puppy dog look as he waited for her answer.

Sam looked around the room. There had to be hundreds if not thousands of flowers. No one had ever done anything so extraordinary for her, and she imagined that Brent had much more up his sleeves. It would be scary opening her heart again, but wouldn't it be worse if she turned him away?

"What'd she say?" Norma's voice carried out from the kitchen.

"She hasn't said anything yet," Brent hollered back, and Sam bit her lip to keep from laughing. Brent's smile stretched across his lips as he continued, "But she's smiling, so I think that's a good sign. Why don't you guys come out here and help me convince her?'"

Fanny stepped out from the kitchen, followed by Norma and Paul. "So, are you?" Fanny continued.

"I'm going to assume there is no truck to fix." Sam dodged the question and looked at her friends.

The elderly woman rolled her eyes good-naturedly. "It's called a ruse, woman. Now answer the question. Are you two dating? Because if you pass on him, I might have to scoop him up myself."

The small gathering laughed, and Sam turned back to Brent. "I don't know. Are we?" Her whole body tingled as she awaited his answer.

"I'd sure like to."

"Me too."

"Then kiss her already." Norma's voice broke their moment, earning a chuckle from both Sam and Brent.

"It would be rude not to, since she's our host." Brent's voice was deep and husky as he lowered his face.

"Yeah, I guess you're right." Sam closed her eyes and turned her face up to meet his.

As his lips touched hers, a shock of electricity traveled down her spine.

The friends behind them clapped and cheered, but Sam's focus remained on Brent. When he pulled back, she smiled up at him. She was finally excited for the future for the first time since arriving in Soda Spurs.

"This will be great publicity." Julia's voice broke the

moment. She had her phone pointed at them and was rapidly clicking what Sam assumed was the camera button

Everyone in the restaurant turned simultaneously to her.

"What? He's a star, and he needs to sell his movies. People love a Cinderella story. They will eat this up."

Norma stared at Julia for a minute, a dumbfounded expression on her face. Then she shook her head and turned back to the rest of the group. "Well, I think this calls for pie."

"I'm always up for pie," Paul said.

Brent and Sam smiled at each other. Sam didn't feel the need for pie, but she wouldn't pass down the opportunity to spend more time with Brent.

"You should have the apple. It's delicious." Brent smiled as he pulled her to the bar.

She swatted his arm playfully. "I know that. I live here, remember?"

"I'll have a slice of apple too," Fanny said loudly, "and a big scoop of ice cream."

"Do you have any gluten free pie?" Julia asked as she inspected a barstool before gingerly sitting.

Norma's deep laugh filled the room. "Honey, round here we don't even know what gluten is."

Julia's face flushed red. "Oh, well, then maybe just a coffee," she stumbled. Pausing, she looked around the small room. "Do you have a cappuccino maker?"

"Is she for real?" Norma asked Brent.

Brent shrugged his shoulders and shook his head. "City dwellers. What can I say?"

Laughter ensued again as Norma rolled her eyes and turned to get the pie. Sam took a moment to survey the motley crew. A meddling older woman, a redneck farmer, an uptight agent, a lively cook, herself, and Brent. Before today she would have classified him as a city slicker, but he seemed to be morphing into small town charm right before her eyes. Sam smiled as she thought about how God could unite even the most opposite of people and make something beautiful.

*Thank you, God for your sense of humor*, she thought as Norma returned with plates laden with pie. *And thank you for this family, as odd as it might be.*

Brent turned her direction and flashed a wink before digging into his slice of pie, and Sam's heart fluttered as she thought of the blissful future ahead of them.

# CHAPTER 15

"Come on." Brent tapped his heel in feigned agitation. It was Thursday evening, and had to get to Houston tonight to make his meeting in the morning, but he wasn't in a hurry for that reason.

"It would help if you told me where we were going," Sam hollered from her closet. "I mean I would dress differently for Marnie's than Ernesto's."

"If I told you that, it wouldn't be a surprise." Brent looked down at his watch. If they didn't hurry, they might miss his surprise and then his agitation would be real. "Just pick something nice. You look beautiful in anything."

Sam emerged from the closet wearing a simple black dress, which she tugged and pulled on, revealing her uncomfortableness.

Brent let out a low whistle. "Wow, you look amazing."

Pink flooded Sam's cheeks. "I feel overdressed."

"It's only because you're used to greasy coveralls and jeans," Brent laughed, taking her hand and pulling her close. "You look great." He placed a quick kiss on her lips before pulling her toward the front door.

"Wait." She placed a splayed hand on his chest. "I need my truck keys."

He shook his head and smiled down at her. "No keys tonight. You're not driving."

"Um, you don't have a car, remember? You totaled it right after I fixed it. Not cool by the way." She swatted his arm playfully.

"Well, I had to find some reason to see you again," Brent returned.

"Haha." Sam's smile turned serious. "Never do that again though."

"I promise; now come on." Brent opened the front door and enjoyed the gasp that escaped from Sam's lips as she spied the stretch limo he had ordered.

"We're taking a limo into Soda Spurs?" she asked. "Don't you think that's a little showy?"

Brent chuckled. "We're not eating in Soda Spurs, Sam." He waited while she locked the front door, and then took her hand again as he helped her down the stairs.

Sam shook her head, but she smiled as he opened the limo door and helped her inside. "I have to ask, aren't you supposed to be heading back to Houston tonight?"

Brent climbed in beside her and closed the door. "Don't worry, there's plenty of time after dinner." He pursed his lips together to keep from smiling and giving away his secret.

"Can I ask you something else?" When he nodded, she continued. "Julia mentioned your family wouldn't have come to the hospital. Can I ask what happened between you?"

Brent sighed. "We were always wealthy, but my father believed in a strong work ethic. When I told him I wanted to be a writer, he wasn't pleased. He wanted me to work on wall street or something a little more stable. So, I moved to Los Angeles and that was the last we spoke."

"I'm so sorry, Brent." Sam laid a hand on his arm and stared at him with glistening eyes.

"Thank you, but tonight isn't about sadness. Tonight is about new beginnings." He wrapped his arm around Sam and pulled her closer, enjoying the sweet smell of her shampoo.

Half an hour later, the limo stopped and the driver opened the door. Brent climbed out first and held his hand out to Sam. Her eyes widened as she took in the surroundings. "I don't understand. I thought we were having dinner."

"Oh, we're going to have dinner." Brent bit the inside of his lip to keep his smile from stretching across his face. "But not here." He took her hand and led her up the red carpet. "I need to get a new car. I thought we'd eat on the plane on the way to Houston and then you could help me pick out my next car. I know a car isn't a necessity in Soda

Spurs, but I don't like being without one, and I really miss driving."

"Won't they be closed by the time we get there?" Sam asked, glancing at her watch.

"Maybe for the general public."

"But you're not the general public," Sam said slowly.

"No, I am not. Now, come on. Your dinner awaits milady."

Sam laughed as he led her up the steps of the airplane. "Will we be returning tonight?"

Brent shook his head. "No, since I have my meeting in Houston tomorrow, I thought this would be a perfect time to show you around. I'll take you to your hotel after the dealership."

"But I didn't pack anything," Sam protested.

"Already been taken care of."

"But the shop," Sam continued.

"Also taken care of. Don't worry, Sam. I have this all covered. Now, come on. I'm starving."

~

"Good evening, sir, mademoiselle."

The words were uttered by a woman in a pressed black skirt and white shirt who stood just inside the plane. Her blond hair was curled into a knot at the nape of her neck.

Brent issued a thank you as they passed her.

Sam nodded a hello at the woman, but her eyes were taking in the insides of the Learjet. She had never been on a private plane before. Instead of the several tight rows of seats, there were only eight spacious seats. Four seats had their backs to Sam and four faced her. A large empty space existed in between the two front rows, but a table draped in a white tablecloth and sporting china and a vase of roses filled the space.

"Do you always travel like this?" Sam asked Brent. Awe was the only emotion she could feel and it overwhelmed her.

Brent chuckled a deep resonating sound. "Of course. What's the point of having money if you don't use it. Sometimes I drive though, but that's on hold until I get a new car."

He led her to the table and helped her into one of the seats before sitting across from her.

"My name is Monica, and I'll be your waitress and stewardess today. Our flight will be a short flight, but plenty of time for you to enjoy our petite sirloin and fingerling potatoes."

Monica turned and disappeared down the aisle and Sam smiled at Brent. "This is more than you needed to do to impress me."

"Maybe, but you deserve it."

Sam glanced out the window as the plane began to move. She hadn't flown often, but enough to remember the funny sensation that erupted in her stomach when the plane began gathering speed. Sam felt no such sensation this time. The takeoff was so smooth, she wouldn't have even known they had lifted off if she hadn't been watching out of the window.

Monica reappeared a moment later carrying a tray that held a bread basket, two plates of food, and two wine glasses with a sparkling red liquid that sloshed gently against the sides of the glasses as she adjusted the tray.

She placed a glass in front of each of them, followed by the plate of food, and finally the basket of bread in the middle. The sweet smell of the meat glided up to Sam's nose and set her mouth watering.

"Let me know if you need anything else," Monica said before disappearing again.

"Shall we pray?" Brent asked.

Sam could only nod. She was still amazed by the situation. Was this what dating Brent would be like? She closed her eyes and listened to his melodic voice as he thanked God for the food and the many blessings he had been given. Sam felt blessed as well. She might not have Brent's money, but it appeared she had a Christian man who was willing to focus on God with her. What more could she ask for?

After Brent finished with an 'amen,' Sam dug into the food. There was a ravenous hole in her stomach yearning to be fed. She didn't usually skip meals, but she had been so focused on work and trying to earn enough to keep the shop open that she hadn't even thought to eat until just before Brent showed up for their date.

Sam wasn't sure whether it was the food or the hunger burning inside her, but as she chewed the first bite of steak, she decided she had never had a finer one. The meat was crispy on the outside and coated with some smoky glaze, and the inside was soft and flavorful.

"This is amazing," she uttered between bites.

"Well, I couldn't very well take you on a plane and serve subpar food, could I?" he asked with a smile. "I'm glad you like it though. You deserve the royal treatment, Sam."

As the heat crawled up her neck, Sam wondered if she could live like this. She had grown up in a simple home. Plenty of food on the table and a roof over their heads, but she had never been able to take dance or gymnastics growing up due to the lack of money. Sam had never felt like anything was lacking though as her parents had filled the gaps with love, but now she wondered if life would ever be the same. Could you live with money like this and then go back to none? Would Brent ever be truly happy in Soda Spurs?

Sam kept the questions to herself, not wanting to ruin the night. There would be plenty of time to ask them later.

∾

*B*rent felt like a kid at Christmas as the limo pulled up to the North Houston Porsche dealership. He couldn't wait to have Sam help him pick out a new car. Truth was, he could have just ordered the car he wanted. Pierre, the owner, would know what he liked. But Sam was a mechanic, and even though she didn't often work on Porsches, he thought she might enjoy seeing them, hearing them, maybe even test driving one.

He held the limo door open for her and smiled when her eyes grew round as she climbed out of the limo.

"Is this a dealership or a whole city?"

Brent chuckled. The building was huge-two stories with a showroom that typically displayed two dozen cars. Yellows and reds from the setting sun glistened off the white building. "Come on."

The dealership was officially closed for the evening, but as promised, Pierre had the side door unlocked.

"We're sneaking in?" Sam asked.

"We're getting special treatment," Brent replied as he opened the door.

The room opened into a large showroom. An expansive white desk stretched across the room and the white marble floor glistened as if it had just been cleaned.

"Ah, you made it. Good to see you my friend." Pierre stood from behind the desk. He walked over to greet them, his Italian loafers clicking on the marble flooring. His short black hair perfectly matched the color of his expensive suit.

"Thanks for staying open, Pierre." Brent shook the man's outstretched hand. "This is my girlfriend, Sam."

Pierre's eyes flicked to Sam, and he brought her hand to his lips, laying a soft kiss on the back. "She is too pretty for you."

Brent chuckled and gazed at Sam. "Don't I know it, but don't let her good looks fool you. Sam here is an amazing mechanic and will probably spend more time looking under the hood than admiring the exterior of the cars."

Pierre's eyes widened. "Beautiful and smart? Now I know she's too good for you. Why don't you drop this fool and come work for me?"

A soft blush spread across Sam's cheeks. "While that is a very tempting offer, I'm kind of fond of Brent here."

"Ah, well, I can't blame you there. Brent is a good man. Now, what would you like to see first?" Pierre asked.

Brent turned to Sam. Though he was the one shopping, he wanted her to be able to see a car she wanted.

"Can I see a Carrera?" she asked. "I've always loved the look of them."

"She has good taste too." Pierre flashed Brent a smile as he led them over to the cars. At least a dozen filled the room, ranging in colors and designs. "Here it is, the brand-new Carrera."

Sam's eyes shone as she ran her hand over the smooth red paint. "Wow, I never thought I'd see one this close."

"Why don't you get inside?" Brent asked. "See how it feels?"

She turned wide eyes to Pierre, as if asking for permission.

"Yes, please." Pierre waved his hand at her to indicate it was fine.

Brent noticed Sam's hand was shaking just slightly as she opened the door and slid into the driver seat. Her hands glided over the steering wheel with a soft touch, and her mouth parted. Though he figured she wouldn't allow him to right now, Brent promised that one day he would purchase a Carrera for her.

## CHAPTER 16

"*A*re you really going to be happy with a Boxster?" Sam asked as they left the dealership. Brent had decided on a silver Boxster, and while nice, it wouldn't have been Sam's first choice.

Brent took her hand and laced his fingers with hers as they walked back to the limo. "Julia read me all the statistics of red cars and accidents while I was in the hospital. She might have skinned me alive if I bought another red car."

"I know, but a Boxster?" Sam was kidding and she knew Brent understood that by the look he gave her.

"Get in and stop giving me grief woman." He motioned her inside the door to the limo. The driver, clad all in black with a white shirt held the door open. Though Brent had paid for the Porsche outright and they could have driven it home, he was still sore from the accident and Sam did not feel comfortable driving such an expensive car around in a city she didn't know. So, Brent had opted to have it delivered and hired another limo pickup.

When the driver climbed into the front seat, Brent leaned forward to speak through the window. "To the St. Regis, please."

"Right away, sir."

"Are you still hungry?" Brent began opening cabinets and the mini fridge. "There's nuts and champagne."

Sam laughed at the image of him scrounging in the limo. "I'm fine. Overwhelmed actually. This is …."

"It does take some getting used to," he agreed, "but it has some nice perks."

Sam nodded and ran her hand across the plush leather seat. Had she ever been in a limousine? Maybe in high school. Prom. Yes, definitely Prom. Connor, her boyfriend at the time, and the other boys had gone in on a limo to take them to prom, but it wasn't the same. That limo had been older, the seats upholstered in some knobby fabric instead of the smooth leather caressing her palms now. And with ten of them shoved inside, it definitely hadn't felt as spacious.

"What are you thinking?"

Sam blinked and focused on Brent who was staring intently at her. "Oh, I was just thinking back to high school - the only other time I was in a limo - and wondering if I'm really cut out for your world."

Brent picked up her hand and ran his thumb across the top. He was silent for a moment. Gathering his thoughts?

"Sam, I enjoy having money, but it doesn't define me. I grew up in a small town, and even though my family was well off, my father hid how wealthy we were until I was a teenager. It might be an adjustment, but I could go back to that life."

Sam stared into his eyes, gauging his truthfulness. His eyes met her gaze, and they were open and honest. Perhaps he could adjust to living in a smaller town again, but could she ask him to?

As the limo pulled to a stop, the driver turned to face them. "Here we are, sir. Let me get the door for you."

Brent stepped out first and held his hand out to Sam. As she took in the multilevel, white building, her eyes widened. Lush green trees surrounded the building, which meant it was obviously watered a lot as there wasn't much rain in Houston.

"It's so...."

"Big?" he suggested.

"Opulent was the word I was going for. I don't think I've ever stayed in a hotel so large."

A large smile spread across Brent's face, showing off his white teeth. "Just wait until you see the inside." He pressed a few bills into the driver's hand, then took Sam's hand and led her inside.

Brent hadn't been joking about the inside. The floor

was a white marble, but it was threaded with gold. Golds, browns, and reds accented the room. The couches were tan and gold. The rugs brown and red. A gold speckling covered the white marble desk that lay in front of them. A light brown wainscoting covered the walls and the ceilings were painted a beige color and had to be at least twelve feet high.

In the middle of the ceiling, a large gold chandelier hung down, sending prisms of color across the floor. Sam's eyes flitted from one piece of the room to the next, unsure of what to focus on.

Brent led the way to the large desk and greeted the woman behind it. "Hello, Brent McKasson checking in."

"Yes, Mr. McKasson. Welcome to the St. Regis. Are you having a nice evening tonight?" The woman was young, in her late twenties probably with shoulder length brown hair and big doe eyes that she batted occasionally at Brent as she checked him in.

*I'm standing right here,* Sam thought, but she wasn't flashy. Yes, her dress was nice, but still probably nothing anyone in this hotel would touch. And her soft dark hair framed her face nicely, but there was nothing stellar about it or her blue eyes. Sam bit her lip, not enjoying this feeling of insecurity.

"Have a nice stay," the woman's voice finished.

"Thank you. We will." Brent emphasized the "we" and squeezed Sam's hand, lifting it slightly to bring it into the woman's vision.

"Why did you do that?" Sam hissed as he led her to the elevator. "You're not staying with me."

He pressed the button, and the gold doors slid open. "No, but she doesn't know that. I didn't like the way she was looking at me, like I was her next meal or something." He pretended to shudder as he stepped into the elevator, but his smile gave him away.

Sam's mouth dropped open. "You like the attention," she accused as she joined him. The doors closed, and Brent punched the highest button.

"No, I used to, but you showed me that I want so much more. While the attention is flattering, I also wanted her to know that I was taken."

The heat crept up Sam's neck again. How did he always know what to say?

With a soft ding, the elevators doors hissed open, and they stepped out. There was a door to the left and a door to the right, but not much else in this hallway. Brent turned left and flashed the card key across the reader. A soft click sounded, and the door swung inward.

"You got the penthouse?" Sam's eyes widened as she stepped inside. "This isn't a hotel room, Brent. It's an entire apartment, and it's bigger than my house back home."

Brent just smiled and continued inside. The room opened into a large sitting room with a couch, two chairs, and fireplace. To the left was a door leading to the bedroom and bathroom and to the right was a small kitchen and eating area.

"I figured since you would be here a few days, you deserved more than a hotel room," Brent said.

"But Brent, you didn't let me pack. I don't have any clothes or my toothbrush." Although Sam was certain a place like this would give you a toothbrush and toothpaste.

"Don't worry about it. Julia took care of everything." He led the way to the bedroom and flicked the light on. A large king-sized bed filled the room and on top of the bed was a plethora of clothing. Shirts, pants, skirts, socks, and a bag from Victoria's Secrets which undoubtedly held undergarments. "Size six, right?"

Sam nodded as she stepped up to the bed. Though all the price tags had been taken off, Sam was certain everything on the bed was brand new. "What is all this?"

"I told Julia to buy you a few pieces you would feel comfortable in." Brent chuckled as he looked over the clothes. Though nice, they were definitely not what Sam usually wore. "As you can see, she isn't sold on your style and was obviously hoping to influence you a little. You'll find all the bathroom necessities you need stocked as well."

"I'm only here for a few days," Sam stammered. "Why would you go through all this for a few days?"

"Because you're worth it," Brent pulled her close and cupped her face with his hand, "and I want you to feel comfortable here."

As his lips closed on hers, explosions fired in Sam's

head. She hoped it wasn't just the money, but she was afraid she was falling for Brent. Hard and fast.

~

*B*rent opened the door of his penthouse apartment located just a few minutes from the St. Regis hotel and sighed slightly. He had only been gone a week, but he had missed the place. Actually, it wasn't so much the place as the space. Sam was a hospitable host, but he had been staying in a single room with a bathroom down the hall. After he left the hospital and returned to Sam, he had stayed with Fanny in an even smaller room with a shared bathroom. They hadn't thought it would be appropriate for him to stay with Sam again now that they were dating. Either way, both were quite a stretch from his two thousand square foot apartment.

He took a moment to wander the rooms and re-acquaint himself with the place. Though it was just him, the apartment boasted three bedrooms, two bathrooms, a formal and informal living room, a large kitchen, and a dining room. Brent paused for a moment outside his bedroom as his king-sized bed called to him, but he needed to unwind first.

He returned to the kitchen and grabbed a drink from the fridge before wandering into the living room. A little TV, that's what he needed. Something trivial he could watch and just unplug. Brent had just settled into his favorite recliner when a knock sounded at the door. He glanced at his watch, surprised that someone would be at his door this late, but he rose and crossed to the door.

The minute he opened the door, he cursed himself for not using the spyhole first. Tricia stood on the other side of the door, dressed to the nines. Her glossy red lips pulled into a smile as her gaze met his.

"What are you doing here, Tricia?" He positioned himself in the doorway to block her entrance.

"Giving you another chance." Her voice sounded more like a purr as she laid a hand on his arm. "I think you were confused last time when I came to the cabin."

"I wasn't confused, Tricia. Not last time or the other times I broke it off. I want something different. Something you can't offer me."

Tricia's lips pushed out in a pout, and she batted her eyes at him. "I can be anything you want. Just tell me what you want me to be."

Brent sighed and rolled his eyes. "That's just it, Tricia. I don't want to have to tell you what to be. Sam just is what I want."

Tricia's eyes widened into large saucers. "Sam? Who's Sam? Is she the one you were jabbering about at the cabin? You can't be serious Brent. You'll never be happy in that tiny town."

"I already am happy, Tricia. Look, I'm sorry it didn't work out, but you'll find someone who suits you better. It just won't be me."

Tricia's gaze turned into a hateful glare. "You're the one who will be sorry, Brent. You have no idea what I'm capable of."

Before he could say another word, she whirled and stomped away. With a shake of his head, Brent shut the door. Tricia might be crazy, but he was pretty sure she was harmless. Still, he was glad to be rid of her. He made a mental note to ask the management to keep her from coming to his room again.

# CHAPTER 17

*S*am woke up the next morning feeling like a princess. The large bed had sucked her in the night before causing her to fall asleep just minutes after her eyes closed. Now, as the sun peeked in through the lacy curtains, Sam stretched and enjoyed the satiny caresses of the sheets against her bare skin. Had she ever slept on satin sheets in the past? She couldn't remember a time, but she thought she might need to purchase some for her bed back home.

After a final stretch, Sam tossed back the comforter and swung her legs out of bed. Her feet sank into the plush carpet as she crossed the room and grabbed the terry cloth robe from the back of the door. She was hungry, but she had no idea what to do for breakfast. Brent hadn't let her pack anything, and she certainly couldn't afford room service.

As if on cue, her cell phone rang and Brent's cell number flashed on the screen. With a smile, she punched the call button. "Hello?"

"Good morning." His voice was warm on the other end. "How did you sleep?"

"Very well and you?"

Brent laughed. "I can't deny that I missed my bed. It was a good night's sleep for sure. I have my meeting this morning, but I wanted to tell you to order some room service and charge it to the tab…"

"Brent, I can't do that," Sam interrupted.

"Yes, you can. Order some room service. Enjoy a massage or spa treatment if you want. I should be done by around five. I'll come pick you up and we'll have dinner."

"Okay, that sounds good. I'll see you then." Sam clicked the end button and sighed. There was no point in quibbling over the money. He had planned this trip, and though Sam wanted to chip in, she knew he would not let her. She would do nothing extravagant, but at least she could order some breakfast and maybe see about a massage.

The room service menu was on a table near the bed and after scanning the options, Sam decided on an omelet with a side of fresh fruit and coffee. She placed the order and then padded into the living room.

A big screen TV hung on one wall. Sam clicked on the remote and curled up in a chair to wait for the food.

The knock sounded a few minutes later, and Sam rose

to open the door. A woman in black pants and a white shirt smiled at her from the other side. In her hands was a large tray topped with a golden cover.

"Hi, I have breakfast."

"Thank you." Sam stepped back to allow entrance and pointed to an end table. "You can put it there on the table."

The woman nodded, but even as she walked to the table, her eyes kept returning to Sam. The woman's gaze made Sam feel like she was an animal at an exhibit. "I'm sorry, it's just that you look so familiar to me."

Sam shook her head. She was no one famous. "You must have me confused with someone else. I don't live here. I live in a pretty small town, and I'm a mechanic. No one famous."

Suddenly, the woman's eyes lit up and she snapped her fingers. "That's it. You're dating Brent McKasson, right?"

Sam blinked, unsure how this woman would know that. "I am, but how…"

"You guys were on the cover of the Style section this morning. I read it every week because I have no life. I mean I'm nearly twenty-five and still working here."

"Oh, well, I'm sure you have a life," Sam began but the woman cut her off.

"I can't wait to tell all my friends I met you." Her eyes widened and she grabbed Sam's arm. "What's it like dating a billionaire? I bet he takes you to exotic places and buys you tons of expensive jewelry? Do you have any jewelry?" She turned Sam's hand over searching for rings or Rolexes, Sam wasn't sure which.

As tactfully as possible, Sam removed her hand. "We've only just begun dating, so there's been no jewelry, and this is the only trip we've taken together. Honestly, I'm just here for a few days while he attends some meeting, and then I'll be going back to Soda Spurs."

The woman's eyes fell. "Well, that's not much of a story to tell. Hope you enjoy your breakfast."

She turned and exited but as she did, Sam heard her mumble under breath, "Bet that relationship won't last long."

As the woman pulled the door shut, Sam sighed and leaned into the couch. What if the woman was right? What if she was too boring for Brent?

~

*B*rent checked his watch as he got out of the limo. He hoped this meeting wouldn't last long as he had plans to take Sam on a romantic dinner cruise.

"Way to cut it close," Julia said as he reached the front door where she was waiting. "You know they hate being kept waiting."

Brent winked at her and tapped his watch. "And I have five minutes to spare. You worry too much."

Julia rolled her eyes. "Let's just go."

Brent followed her into the atrium and down a long

hallway to her office. As the production company was based in Los Angeles, this meeting would be happening over webcam.

"Welcome Mr. McKasson, Ms. Adams." The president's face filled the large TV screen on the wall. "Thank you for coming."

"Always willing to meet with Night Ranger producers." Julia took one empty chair and Brent took one beside her.

"We'll cut right to the chase since our time is valuable as I'm sure yours is. We want to get filming on the next movie right away. Night Ranger four made more money than we even planned, so the writers are hard at work on the next three movies."

"Wait, I'm sorry," Brent interrupted. "Did you say three more movies?"

"Is that a problem?" the president asked. One eyebrow arched higher than the other on his face as he leaned even closer to the camera, filling up even more of the screen in front of Brent. Beside him, Julia shot him a glare which Brent ignored.

"Well, it might be. Look, I appreciate the opportunity you gave me with Night Ranger, and I have certainly appreciated the money, but I've been wanting to do something different for a while now. This last weekend, I began writing a script. I don't know if it will turn into anything, but I'd like to take some time off to finish it."

"I'm sorry." Julia jumped in. "Brent was involved in an

automobile accident a few days ago, and I'm afraid he may not be thinking straight."

"I'm thinking fine." Brent suddenly wondered if he even wanted to keep acting. He was tired of people pushing him to take rolls he didn't want just for the money. He hadn't realized how unhappy he'd been until Sam had shown him how happy he could be. And the return to a small town and reminded him of the simple things he missed. Things like people knowing your name because they knew you and not just because they saw you on a movie screen. "I'm just asking for a break. Maybe I'll feel like doing more Night Rangers in the future, but I just don't have it in me right now."

"I see. Well, I can put a hold on the movie for a few months, but if you are still unsure by the end of summer, we will have to find a new Derek McCloud."

"Absolutely, sir. I understand."

"Best of luck then, and be sure to let me know what you decide." With that the image clicked out and the screen went blank.

"What are you doing?" Julia hissed at him.

"Julia, I told you I was getting tired of Night Ranger. I want something that will stretch me and make me a better actor. So, find me something like that or it might be time for me to retire."

"It's this girl, isn't it?" Julia asked. "She's bewitched you."

Brent chuckled. "I don't know if I'd go so far as

bewitched, but captivated me? Absolutely. I haven't been this happy since Rachel died, and I thought you'd be happy for me."

"I am, but Brent, Night Ranger made you who you are."

"Well, it's time I reinvent myself. Now, I'm taking Sam out on the town. Let me know when you have a real role for me." Brent felt a little bad leaving Julia staring after him with her mouth open, but he was finally ready to move on to something better. And if something better didn't present itself then he had a story of his own to finish.

~

Sam cringed when the knock sounded at the door. She couldn't handle one more person asking for her autograph or the story of her and Brent, but as she peeked through the spyhole - she had learned to start doing that after the third story seeker - her mood lifted. It was Brent, and she'd never been so happy to see someone in her life.

She flung open the door and rushed into his arms.

"Well, not quite the reaction I expected, but definitely one I enjoy." Brent circled his arms around her.

She pulled him in and shut the door. "It's been crazy today. The waitress who brought my breakfast recognized me from our picture in the paper."

"What picture?" he asked.

Sam chuckled. So, he'd had no idea either. "I'll get to that. Anyway, the waitress must have told everyone she knew because I've had a steady stream of people knocking on the door asking for my autograph or the story of how we met or what it's like to date a billionaire. One of them actually brought the paper with our picture in, which I kept before ushering her out." Sam walked over to the table and picked up the newspaper. "Evidently we made the style section."

Brent's eyes widened as he took in the picture of them kissing at Norma's. "Sam, I'm so sorry. I had no idea Julia would send this out to be published."

"It's okay. It comes with the territory, right?" Sam wanted him to say no, that this was unusual, that his girlfriends weren't routinely hounded by photographers, but she knew that wasn't the case. Just as she knew that she had been fooling herself. She wasn't cut out for his life. She didn't want to be in newspapers or on TV. She just wanted a simple life in a small town.

"Yeah, it does. Still, I'm sorry you had to go through that."

"Brent, I think we made a mistake. I'm not a spotlight kind of girl. I don't want my picture taken every time I go outside. I just want to go home."

"Then I'll give it up."

Sam shook her head. "I can't ask you to do that."

He took her hands, and his stare was honest and frank as he gazed into her eyes. "You aren't. I'm offering."

"And that's sweet, but I can't let you do that either. Look, Brent, it was great in Soda Spurs, but that's not who you are. This," she motioned to the grand room, "this is who you are. Besides, it's only been a week. I can't let you give everything up for me when we don't even know if we'd last."

His shoulders sank and defeat covered his face. "Are you sure? I can fly back and forth."

"But I'd still be in your limelight. And reporters would still be hounding me. One came to the shop Monday after you'd left town. There would be more if we were dating. I know some women would kill for that attention, but it's not for me."

Brent nodded though he didn't look convinced. "Okay, if that's what you want, then I'll take you home."

"It is." But even as the words left her lips, Sam knew she would regret them.

# CHAPTER 18

"*B*rent? Did you hear what I said?" Julia asked.

"What?" He looked up from the script he had been reading over. It wasn't awful, but it still didn't have the depth he was looking for.

She sighed clearly agitated she was having to repeat herself. "Twentieth Century Fox called and they want you to audition for a role in the next X-men movie."

Brent shook his head. "No, I told you no more action movies."

Julia raised an eyebrow at him. "What are you still doing here, Brent? It is clear your head and your heart are somewhere else. You've done nothing but mope and turn down every script I've gotten for you."

"It's just…" Brent shrugged. "Nothing feels right."

"Nothing feels right because you don't have Sam. I

didn't think it was possible since you'd only known the woman a week, but it is obvious you're in love with her."

Brent's head dropped onto his palm. "I know, but what am I going to do about it? She told me it wouldn't work out, that she didn't want me to return with her."

"She told you that because she didn't want you to regret giving up fame and fortune for her, but I don't think this life appeals to you any longer. Have you even continued writing your story?"

"No, not since Sam left."

"Then that's what you need to do. Step out of the limelight. Go back to Sulphur Springs or wherever it is Sam lives. Win her back and finish your story. I never thought I'd say this, but I think it what's you need to do."

Brent's head popped up and for the first time in a week, hope flooded his veins. "Do you think that will work? What if she won't take me back?"

Julia rolled her eyes. "Do some grand gesture she can't refuse. You have the money, and she's probably just as miserable as you are anyway."

Grand gesture. Yes, he could do that. He just needed to figure out what the perfect grand gesture would be. "Thanks, Julia." He pushed back the chair and crossed the room to place a kiss on her cheek. "You've been amazing."

A blush colored her cheeks and she shook her head. "Just invite me to the wedding."

"I will."

∽

*S*am stared at the picture of Brent on the TV and sighed. What had she been thinking breaking it off? She had been nothing but miserable the last week, spending her evenings binge watching the Night Ranger movies. The only good thing that had happened was that her short stint of fame had brought new customers to the shop. If it kept up, she'd have enough money to cover rent for the next few months, but what good was that if she was miserable?

A knock sounded at her door and Sam put the tub of ice cream she had been eating from on the table beside her before crossing to the door. No need to broadcast her depression to whoever was on the other side.

She opened the door and blinked in surprise. Fanny stood in the doorway. Sam had never seen her anywhere other than her own front porch. "Hi, Fanny, what can I do for you?"

"Nothing." The old woman pushed past Sam and into the house. "It's what I can do for you."

"What are you talking about?" Sam asked. Though she hadn't invited the woman in, she shut the door and turned to her guest.

"You've been moping around for the last week. Norma says you aren't eating much either." She looked around the room which Sam hadn't bothered to pick up. Her tongue clicked as her eyes landed on the ice cream container. "And ice cream doesn't count."

Embarrassed, Sam grabbed the container and shoved the lid back on. Then she walked into the kitchen and placed it back in the freezer. She jumped in surprise when she turned around and Fanny was right behind her. The woman was stealthy.

"I waited to see if you would come to your senses, but since it appears you aren't, I'm here to help you out."

"Come to my senses about what?" Sam asked.

"About Brent, you silly woman. I'm not sure what you were thinking breaking it off, but it's clear you care about him. Now, I lost my poor Frank ten years ago and not a day goes by that I don't miss him. I'm not going to let the two of you waste precious time when it's clear you belong together." Her finger poked Sam's chest as she punctuated the last three words.

Sam sighed. "What am I supposed to do, Fanny? I broke it off with him. He's probably moved on by now anyway."

"You really are stubborn, aren't you? That man clearly loves you. Did you not see what he did to Norma's diner?"

"Yes, but that was before." Why was she protesting so much? She knew in her heart Brent hadn't moved on. No man made a huge gesture like that if he didn't care at least a little.

"And this is now. So, here's what you do. You are going to pack and drive to Houston and tell him you were wrong. Paul can cover the shop for a few days, and I'll check on the house."

"Fanny, I can't just pack up and leave," Sam protested.

"Yes, you can, and I'm here to help."

Indecision filled Sam. She did want to see Brent again, but would he want to see her? If he did, wouldn't he have called? However, she had been the one to break it off, so maybe he was just honoring her wishes. An impulsive desire to follow Fanny's advice filled her. "Okay. Let's pack."

They had just finished packing her suitcase when a knock sounded at the door. Sam glanced up at the older woman. "Are we expecting someone else?"

Fanny's white hair bounced slightly as she shook her head. "Don't look at me. I did my part."

Sam rolled her eyes and walked the short hallway to the front door. For the second time that evening, she pulled it open and blinked in surprise. "Brent?"

"I know you said it wouldn't work, but Sam, I don't want to stay there without you."

Fanny entered the living room then pulling Sam's suitcase behind her.

Brent's eyes flitted to the suitcase and back to Sam. "Are you going somewhere?"

Sam smiled for the first time in a week. "Yeah, to see you. To tell you I was wrong."

Fanny brushed her hands together in a dusting off motion. "Well, I guess my work here is done. It's good to see you again, Mr. McKasson. I expect I'll be seeing more of the two of you together."

"What was that about?" Brent asked as he watched Fanny walk down the steps.

"Just good friends watching out for each other. Now, come here. We have some lost time to make up for." She wound her arms around his neck and pulled him into the house. As the door clicked shut behind him, she leaned up and met his lips with her own.

# CHAPTER 19

Sam stared at the bill and sighed. Everything had been going so well the last month: Brent had found a rental house to live in until his house was built, business had been steady the first week or so he had been back in town, and of course dating a billionaire came with its own set of benefits. Just yesterday he had rented a helicopter and flown them out to Corpus Christi for the day. She had been too tired to open the mail when they'd gotten home last night, so she'd attacked it this morning and now she wished she hadn't.

A knock sounded at the door. Brent. They were planning to have a late breakfast together, and she wasn't even dressed yet. Sam dropped the bill and hurried to the front door to let him in.

"Good late morning." His eyebrow arched on his forehead. "Is this a new fashion statement?"

Sam swatted his arm. "Come in. I overslept this morning thanks to our late night last night, and then I got caught up catching up on mail. I just need a few minutes."

As Brent wandered to the kitchen, probably for some coffee, Sam scurried into the bedroom. She had just enough time for a quick shower if she hurried, so she turned on the water and then peeled off her clothes.

Fifteen minutes later, Sam re-entered the kitchen, clean and wearing a pink sundress.

"Sam? What is this?" Brent asked, holding up the letter.

Sam sighed. "The landlord is raising my rent at the shop."

Brent shook his head. "Sam, this is double what you were paying. He can't raise it like that."

"It's nothing. I'll take care of it." Sam swiped the letter from his fingers.

"Sam, I can help. I'll talk to him."

"No, I'll do it."

"Why won't you let me help you?" Exasperation colored Brent's voice.

"Because you aren't trying to help. You're trying to take over."

Brent's eyes closed, and he took a deep breath. "Sam, I'm a billionaire. I know that sounds abstract. It does even to me sometimes, but what it means is that I have the money to help you. I have so much money I wouldn't miss the amount to buy your shop and get you some advertising. Imagine what you could do if you got some more clients. Remember how nice it was to be busy?"

Sam did remember. It had been great for a week or two when she and Brent were hot news, but since he had stepped out of the limelight, the press had found other people to follow and they had been forgotten. "Yes, I remember, and I know how much a billion is, Brent. I just... I need to do this on my own. I can't have some man taking care of me."

Brent flinched as if the words had hit him like a punch. "Is that what I am to you? Just some man?"

Sam bit her lip. Those weren't exactly the words she meant, but they had only been dating for a little over a month. She loved him, but she was still scared to rely solely on him. What if she took his money and then they broke up? She would feel like she owed him, and she didn't want to feel indebted to anyone. Not after Greg.

"I thought we were more than that, Sam. I gave up acting for you. I moved here for you. Here." He waved his arm around the room. "Soda Springs. For you."

"I didn't ask you to give up acting or to move here," Sam shot back. "I'm not like your other girlfriends, Brent. You can't just buy my affection." Sam knew she should stop, but she couldn't keep the words from falling out of her mouth.

"I wasn't trying to buy you off." A sadness filled Brent's voice and tugged on Sam's heart. "I took you out yesterday because I wanted to share an amazing day with you, and I'm offering to help you now because I can. And because you are a great mechanic. And because you've been working too hard."

Sam crossed her arms and leaned away from him. "I don't want your help. I was fine before you waltzed into town. I opened this shop by myself and I'll take care of this by myself."

Brent shrugged and rose from the chair. "If that's the way you feel, Sam, then I'll get out of your hair."

They stared at each other. Sam didn't mean the words and she didn't think Brent did either, but neither one of them seemed willing to apologize first.

"You should go," she said, pointing to the door. "I've got work to do."

Brent opened his mouth as if he were going to speak, but Sam folded her arms across her chest and put on her stoic face.

With a sigh, Brent nodded and left her house. Sam fell into the chair and dropped her head into her hands. Why couldn't she just accept help? Why did she always have to push people away?

~

*B*rent left Sam's place unsure exactly where he was going, but knowing he needed to find someone to talk to. He didn't think Sam had meant the words any more than he had, but they were both stubborn and they needed time to cool off. This was the first time they had really argued, and of course it had to be over money.

When he'd first moved to Soda Spurs, Sam had objected the first few dates they'd gone on when he picked up the tab. She had wanted to alternate who paid the check, but there was no way he was doing that. He understood money was tighter for her. It had taken some finagling, but he had finally convinced her that since they were dating, he should be allowed to pick up the check. He loved that she was independent, but he hated it at the same time.

This was bigger though. Brent knew the money from Sam's mother's death had bought most of the equipment, but she'd had to lease the rest, along with the building. She had told him she was barely paying the bills, and now with the increase, the amount was more than Sam was bringing in. Soda Spurs was a small town, and most people walked. There just wasn't enough business for her.

He had more than enough money to buy her shop outright, and he wanted Sam back. Playful Sam who played music trivia with him. Loving Sam who rubbed his shoulders when they were sore from writing. And faithful Sam who prayed with him each night and accompanied him to church on Sunday. She was all these things and more, and he wanted her back.

As he walked away from her house, he found his footsteps leading him to church. Maybe Pastor Ron would be available to talk to. He always seemed to have ideas on how to communicate. Perhaps he could help Brent figure out how to help Sam.

~

Sam watched as the door closed behind Brent and sighed. She hadn't meant to say those words and especially not in that tone. She knew Brent just wanted to help. Like most men, he was a fixer. When he heard a problem, he wanted to fix it.

The problem was, Sam didn't want him to fix it. It would be easy to take his money, but she needed to know she could do this on her own. The only problem was... What if she couldn't? What if there just weren't enough customers in Soda Spurs to keep her garage open. Would she have to move? Or find a new job?

"Lord, I don't know what to do. I really need your guidance."

Only silence answered her. With a sigh, Sam stood and returned to the bedroom. If brunch plans were ruined, she might as well go to the shop and see if she could figure out some way to keep it open.

She quickly changed out of her sundress and into a pair of jeans and a t-shirt. Then she grabbed a banana from the counter and headed out the door.

A small pang of sadness swept over her when she reached the shop and turned the closed sign over to open.

She had hoped when she started her own shop that she would have weekends off, but she'd been coming in the last two Saturdays in hopes of getting more business. Once the reporters had gotten bored of Brent's story and left, the business had died back down too.

No car sat in the empty bay. It had been empty all week. Sam knew she would have to branch out if she wanted to keep the shop open here and that was what she planned to do today. Research affordable options she could branch into.

Sam pulled up the stool behind the counter and turned on the computer. There was a click and a loud whir as the ancient machine struggled to life. Just another thing she would need to update when and if she ever had the money.

The bell above the door jingled, announcing a customer, and Sam lifted her head. "How can I help..." The words died in her mouth as the man in her doorway smiled. She knew that smile. It had swept her off her feet her senior year. It had taken her to prom, and though she hadn't seen the smile in nearly a decade, it had often wandered into her dreams. "Connor?"

"Hi, Sam."

She rose from the stool and blinked as if he were an apparition. Before he left for college, she had thought she and Connor were destined to be together, but the distance had torn them apart as it often did with couples. It was another reason she hadn't agreed to the long-distance relationship Brent had first proposed. She knew firsthand what would have eventually happened. "What are you doing here?"

"I saw your story on TV and couldn't believe my eyes. Car Head Sam Jenkins dating a billionaire movie star. I had to come see if it was true." A look of jocularity poured out of his ocean blue eyes.

Sam had forgotten the power of those mesmerizing blue eyes. "Well, it's true." She rounded the corner to get closer but kept a polite distance. "So, what are you doing now? For work I mean." A red heat flashed across her face as she realized her wording had sounded more like a pick-up line than a curious question.

His blue eyes twinkled at her obvious discomfort, and the smile that stretched across his mouth also accentuated the cleft in his chin. Oh, that cleft. It had been her kryptonite in high school. "I own a car dealership in Dallas."

Sam's jaw fell open. Like herself, Connor had been interested in cars in high school. It was one thing that drew them together, but now he owned his own dealership? She couldn't decide if she was more shocked or jealous. She didn't want to own her own dealership necessarily, but they usually had a shop attached with them and owning that would be amazing. "That's great, Connor, but what are you doing here? Soda Spurs doesn't have a car dealership."

"Oh, I know," he said with a chuckle. "I'm on my way

to a conference, but I had a few days, so I thought I would look you up."

Another heat flare crawled up Sam's neck. "You came out of your way to see me?" The words were small, choked.

"Of course I did. I know we ended abruptly, but the year with you was one of the best of my life and when I saw you on TV? Well, naturally when I knew I was coming near here, I figured I should stop in for a visit."

"I..." Sam shook her head. "I don't know what to say."

"What's it been, Sam? Ten years?" He took a step closer to her, and Sam could almost feel the magnetic energy emanating from him.

"Uh, yeah, close to that I guess." Why was she feeling tongue tied around him? Sure, he was handsome, but they had dated so long ago. She had moved on since then, hadn't she? There had been a few guys in college, Greg, and now Brent. "Well, how have you been? Are you married?"

A dimple appeared in his cheek as he flashed a mischievous smile. "No, guess I haven't found the right woman yet." He took another step toward her.

"Oh, me neither." Sam leaned back as if that might break the power he seemed to have over her. "But I guess you knew that."

His eyes clouded for just a second, then cleared. "Do

you want to get some lunch? As old friends, I mean. I'd love to catch up."

Sam pondered the proposal. She and Brent had parted on angry words this morning which she hated, but it was just lunch. "Sure, let me lock up. We can eat at Norma's. She has pretty good burgers and great pie."

"Sounds good."

❧

"Brent, what can I do for you today?" Pastor Ron asked as he opened his office door. An older, plump man with a full white beard, Pastor Ron looked a lot like Santa Claus and Brent had heard he often dressed up as the jolly man around the holidays.

"I was hoping I could talk to you about Sam."

"Of course, come on in." Pastor Ron stepped back, holding the door open for Brent to enter.

The room wasn't large, but the layout of the desk, couch, and bookcase gave it a homey feel and not a cluttered one. Brent sat on the couch while Pastor Ron rolled the chair out from behind the desk.

"First off," Pastor Ron folded his large frame into the smaller chair, "tell me how you're feeling. No lingering issues?"

Brent nodded as his hand touched his side. There was no pain anymore, but sometimes his hand would creep to the spot and just touch it to be sure. "Yes, sir. I received a clean bill of health at my last check up."

"God is good." Pastor Ron stroked his thick beard. "Okay, so tell me about Sam."

A heavy sigh escaped Brent's lips. "I love her. I think you know that, but she won't let me help her."

"What does she need help with?" Pastor Ron asked, a small smile on his lips. "From what I know of Sam, she is a highly capable woman."

"She is," Brent agreed quickly. "That isn't the issue. It's her shop. Her landlord just raised the rent, and there just isn't enough business here to keep her out of the red."

Pastor Ron nodded, leaned back, and stroked his beard again. A part of Brent was jealous of that beard – he'd never been able to grow a good one – but on the other hand, the few times he had tried, the beard had itched tremendously and driven him crazy.

"And let me guess, you tried to give her money?"

Brent shook his head. It sounded like an inane idea when it came out of Pastor Ron's mouth. "Well, first I offered to talk to the landlord, but then yes, I offered to buy her shop. But only because I really want to help her. Sam has so much talent, and the lack of money is stressing her out."

"Yes, we always want to do that, but would you like me to tell you what I've found in forty years of marriage?"

*What kind of man wouldn't take the advice of someone who had been married that long?* Brent thought with a chuckle. "Of course. Lay it on me."

"Women don't always want help." Pastor Ron folded his hands across his belly as if that were it.

"But I have the money."

"That's wonderful. IF she asks for it. But what she wants right now is just for you to listen."

Brent sighed and bit his bottom lip. "Just listen?"

Pastor Ron nodded. "When she wants your help, she will ask."

"But what if she loses the shop?"

Pastor Ron reached up and stroked his beard. "Sometimes, it takes losing something we love to realize it's okay to ask for help. And remember that God has a plan. If she loses this shop, maybe it will be because he has something better planned for her."

Brent's shoulders rose and fell as he soaked in the wise words. "I don't know how you can have such faith sometimes, Ron, but I will take your advice." It seemed counterintuitive to every part of Brent. If he had the money, why couldn't he help? But he would trust this man he had come to admire over the last few months. The man not only knew his Bible, but after being married so long, he probably knew women a little better than Brent did as well.

"Faith comes with practice, Brent." Pastor Ron stood indicating the end of the conversation. "You may find you have a harder time trusting God because of your money, but remember that He controls even that. What He has given, He can take away. And what He takes away, He can restore."

Brent nodded and shook the pastor's hand, promising he would see him again on Sunday before heading out of the church. Now, only one question remained. Could he sit back and just be a sounding board for Sam?

∼

"Well, this place is… quaint," Connor said after a slight pause.

Sam laughed and placed a hand on his arm. "It may not look like much, but I promise the food is good. Until I met Brent, I pretty much ate every meal here." Sam led him to one of the far tables and they sat down.

"So, this Brent," Connor began, "is it serious?"

"I think so. I mean he moved here to be closer to me." Before she could continue, Norma appeared at their table, and while she didn't say anything, it was clear from her expression that she had questions for Sam.

"Norma, this is a friend of mine from high school, Connor Graham." Sam hoped her introduction would soften Norma's glaring eyes. She had never seen her friend so stiff and unwelcoming.

"Well, we were a little more than friends." Connor grinned as he extended his hand, "but it's nice to meet you all the same."

Norma looked at his outstretched hand but ignored it. "The special today is baked potato soup. I'll be back with waters." She dropped the menus onto the table and spun off. Sam stared after her. She had never seen Norma act this way.

"I don't think your friend likes me." Connor retracted his hand and rubbed it across his chin.

"I'm sure it's not you." Though Sam wasn't sure of that at all. "She's usually so nice and bubbly."

"Maybe just a bad day then." Connor picked up one of the menus and scanned it. He was clearly done with the topic.

"Maybe." Sam glanced Norma's direction again, but the woman had her back turned and was filling glasses. She shook her head and picked up the other menu. Sam didn't really need to read the menu; she knew most of it by heart and what she wanted wasn't on the menu anyway. "Do you know what you want?"

Connor's brow was furrowed as he glanced over the menu. "Honestly, I'm not sure. I've been eating Paleo the last few months, and I'm not sure if any of this would qualify."

There was just a hint of haughtiness in Connor's voice and Sam wondered where it had come from. He had been so down to earth in high school. "Well, I don't know much about Paleo, but I'm sure Norma could make any substitutions you need."

"Perhaps if I just ask her to hold the bread." Connor

laid the menu down, but there was still a slight expression of distaste on his face.

A minute later, Norma was at their table again, placing glasses of water in front of them. She set Connor's glass down harder than necessary and sent water sloshing over the side and onto the table. "My apologies." She grabbed some napkins from her pocket and handed them to Connor.

Sam looked up at Norma again. Though her words had said 'I'm sorry,' her tone definitely hadn't. Norma, however, was avoiding her gaze.

"You ready to order?" Norma asked when Connor had finished mopping up the spilled water.

Connor looked to Sam and gave a slight nod, indicating she should go first.

"I'll have the grilled chicken sandwich with extra avocado." Sam handed her menu back to Norma.

"I didn't see that on the menu." Connor's eyes dropped to the menu again.

"It's not on the menu. It's on the secret menu. Remember, I ate here a lot."

"Well, can I have the same thing without the bread then? Oh, and is there any way you can grill my chicken in coconut oil?"

"Sorry, we only have Crisco around here." Norma took the menu from him.

"Oh, well then I guess it will be fine. I can just work it off later."

Norma issued a curt nod and then turned back to the kitchen.

"Is there a gym in this town?" Connor asked, returning his attention to Sam.

"Yeah, but it's on the other side of town. Are you planning to stay?" Sam asked. "I thought you were just passing through."

"Are you that anxious to get rid of me?" A sly smile played at the corners of Connor's lips.

"What? No," Sam said a little too quickly. "I just thought you were only here for today." Why was he affecting her like this? Making her feel flustered. Was it because of the recent fight with Brent? Or did she have unresolved feelings for Connor?

"I was hoping to at least stay for the day. See you in action."

Sam snorted. "Not much action around here in case you couldn't tell. Soda Spurs is a pretty small place. In fact, I'm not sure you'll get to see me in action. I don't have any customers lined up right now."

Connor's brows furrowed together and he twirled his straw around in his cup. "How are you staying in business then?"

Sam didn't bother trying to stop the sigh that escaped her lips. Her shoulders rolled forward and her eyes dropped to the table top. "To be honest, I'm not. If I don't get some cash soon, I'm going to lose the shop, and then I don't know what I'll do."

"I'm guessing offering you a loan is out of the question," Connor began but Sam's eyes shot up and cut him off. He held up his hands like a peace offering. "Sorry, sore subject I guess."

"Why do you men think throwing money at the problem is the answer?"

Connor chuckled. "Well, in this case, isn't money the answer?"

"You know what I mean." Sam rolled her eyes. "No, I would not take a loan. I wouldn't take Brent's money, and I won't take yours. I'll figure something out."

"What if I could find a way to help you get the money?" Connor asked after a moment.

Norma appeared then and placed the food on the table in front of them. "Thank you, Norma." Sam stared up at her friend hoping to engage the woman and get a clue as to what was bothering her. Norma, however, just issued another nod and turned away. Sam watched her go, determined to talk to her later and find out what was going on.

"Sam."

Connor's voice pulled her attention back to him. "Sorry, what did you ask?"

"What if I could find a way to help you get the money?" Connor repeated.

"I don't want a handout." Sam shook her head. Why did men not understand that sometimes women wanted to work out their own problems?

"Not a handout. Just a friend helping a friend."

Sam regarded Connor. It seemed odd that he would show up out of the blue to see her and then offer a way for her to make the money she needed. On the other hand, she had been praying for a way to get the money. Could Connor be her answer to prayer? "Let's pray over the food, and then you can tell me what you have in mind."

"Uh, sure."

Sam closed her eyes. "Lord, we thank you for this food and for the hands that prepared it. And we thank you for bringing friends back together. Amen."

"Amen," Connor repeated. "So, what if I could offer you a job?"

"A what?" Sam asked before shoving a fry in her mouth.

"A job. My regular mechanic is taking a month sabbatical due to the birth of his baby. I just purchased fifty used cars, and I need someone who can look over them and make sure they are ready to sell. Someone I can trust and who can start right away. It would only be for a few days, maybe a week at most, but I can just about guarantee you would make enough to cover your payment here. Maybe even a few months' worth."

Sam knew that was true. Even her little shop in Dallas had made three times as much as she did now. If he were offering to pay her to check fifty cars, she could easily pull in as much as she needed to pay this month's rent. It wasn't a permanent solution, but it would give her more time.

"Can I have some time to think about it?" Sam asked. "I need to discuss it with Brent too."

"Sure, but I have to tell you I can't hold the job open much longer. I've already interviewed a few good people, and I need to fill it by next week."

Sam nodded as she took a bite of her sandwich. It was a good offer, but something about it just didn't feel right. Her eyes wandered to Norma who was still glaring daggers their direction.

"Excuse me." Sam put her sandwich down. "I'll be right back." She needed to find out what was going on with Norma. When she reached the bar, she leaned in so she could lower her voice and hissed, "What is the matter with you? It's not like you to be rude to a customer."

"What's going on with you?" Norma shot back. "Does Brent know you are having lunch with another man?"

Sam sighed. "No, he doesn't because we had a fight this morning, but Connor's just an old high school friend, Norma. Nothing more." Why did she feel the need to explain herself?

"So, this blast from your past shows up while you are dating a billionaire movie star and you don't find that odd?" Norma's eyes narrowed as she shot another look at Connor.

"No, why would I? It's not like I get any money from

Brent. Connor stated he saw me on TV and was passing by Soda Spurs, so he stopped in."

"I still don't like it." Norma shook her head. "There's just something about him I don't like, but I'll be nicer to him. For your sake."

"Thank you." Sam returned to Connor, but Norma's words cycled through her head. Could Connor have a nefarious reason for seeking her out now?

# CHAPTER 20

*B*rent had just finished paying for the large bouquet of flowers when his phone rang. He shifted the flowers to his left arm and dug the phone out of his pocket with his right. "Hello?"

"Brent, it's Julia. I know you're not acting right now, but I just got word that you're in the running for an action hero award. The ceremony is next week. Do you think you can make it?"

He put the phone between his ear and shoulder so he could flash a wave at Rose before exiting the shop. "Uh, this really isn't a good time right now, Julia."

"It never is, Brent, and this isn't really a request. If you ever finish that story and want it published, you need to stay visible or it will be much harder to get it published. This is a chance to come out for one night, be seen, and stay relevant. You do want it published, don't you?"

"Of course I do."

"Then you need to do this. You know your previous books sold better when you became famous. You're starting to disappear. If you don't stay relevant, it will be much harder to publish. You know how it goes."

Brent nodded though he knew she couldn't see it over the phone. He did need to stay relevant. And this was a great opportunity since it would only be appearing at an award show and not giving up months of his life to be in a film. "Can you give me a day to think about it?" he asked Julia. "I need to discuss the offer with Sam."

"Absolutely, but, Brent, it's a good offer. You really should think about taking it."

"I will." Brent ended the call and slipped the phone back in his pocket. He looked up and realized he was on the edge of town and near Fanny's house.

"When are you going to ask that girl to marry you?" Fanny was in her usual afternoon spot - the rocking chair - with her latest knitting project on her lap, but from the short time he spent with her, Brent knew that she spent her mornings in the kitchen making breakfast, cleaning, and having devotional time. Her evenings were spent in the living room watching reruns of Matlock on TV, but her afternoons were reserved for knitting, the front porch, and the rocking chair.

"Fanny, it's only been a little more than a month." Brent didn't tell her he had been scoping out rings. Online of course. Soda Spurs didn't have a decent jewelry store.

"It only took me a week to know I wanted to marry Frank." Fanny's needles clacked in her weathered hands. Frank was her late husband. He had been dead for ten years, but Fanny still spoke about him as if he were still with her. At first Brent had wondered if Fanny was losing her faculties, but she'd told him it was like talking to Jesus.

"You've got flowers," she continued when Brent didn't answer. "Does that mean you messed up?"

Brent shook his head. "You are an astute woman, Fanny Murphy. Sam and I got in an argument this morning."

"Bout money." Her needles never missed a beat and Brent wondered if she knitted because she needed whatever item she was making or because it was her form of release and relaxation.

Brent chuckled. He shouldn't be surprised Fanny would know all about it. She seemed to know about a lot of things for someone who didn't venture far from her house often. "Yes, about money. How did you know that?"

"Cuz it's always about money when couples fight. Or an ex, and since neither of you have one of those in the picture, I figured it must be about money."

"Well, you're right. I tried to give Sam money, and it didn't go over well, so I'm hoping the flowers help when I apologize tonight."

"You might try wearing a hat too." A tiny grin pulled at the corners of her mouth.

Brent bit back a smile. He should never have told

Fanny about his wish of having a hat the first day he was in town, but she'd weaseled it out of him one afternoon when they were having tea together.

"I don't have one yet, but I'll be sure to get one." With a final wave goodbye, Brent continued to his rental house. Since Sam had probably gone to work after he left and kept the shop open until six, he figured he could use the time working on his story. It was almost done now that he'd returned to Soda Spurs and had his muse back.

As he opened the door to the small house, a sigh escaped his lips. The first thing he had done when he decided to move here was to scope out property and contract a builder, but it would still be another few months before the house he wanted was built.

~

Sam tapped the table as she thought about what to say to Brent. After lunch, she had returned to the shop and thought more about Connor's offer. It seemed to be a good idea even though Norma didn't like him. It wasn't a long-term solution, it would buy her some time.

The knock announcing Brent's arrival sounded on her door. Sam took a deep breath. She was glad he had agreed to still come over after their angry morning words, but now she needed strength.

When she opened the door, the first thing she saw was

not Brent's face, but a large bouquet of colorful flowers. Red roses, daisies, and yellow buttercups filled her vision.

"My apologies, my lady, for trying to fix your problem this morning." Brent held the flowers out and bowed.

Sam chuckled as she took the flowers. "Come in, you silly man."

"Happily." He stepped over the threshold. With one arm, he closed the door behind him, and with the other, he caught Sam about the waist and pulled her to him. "I really am sorry. I had a long talk with Pastor Ron this morning and realized I was trying to fix your problem when all you wanted me to do was listen."

"Thank you." A feeling of renewed adoration swept over Sam. Would he ever cease to amaze her?

"You're welcome." Brent's eyes stared into hers before closing as his face leaned closer. His lips touched hers, sending a tremor of excitement through her.

Sam returned the kiss with every ounce of her being. She had no idea what was going to happen after she told him her plans, so she wanted to enjoy this moment fully.

"Well, I certainly wasn't expecting that," Brent said when they parted. "Maybe we should quarrel more often if this is how we make up."

"Funny." Sam batted his arm as he released her. "I do have news though." She paused and bit her lip as she tried to muster her courage. "Come into the kitchen so I can put these in water."

"I have some news too."

"Really? Do you want to go first?" Sam asked. Now that he was here, she wasn't sure she wanted to tell him. What if he didn't take it well? What if this ended their relationship?

She opened a cabinet and stood on her tiptoes to reach the vase on the top shelf, but her hand was just shy. Brent's form filled the space behind her and he pulled the vase she was reaching for down. Sam tried not to breathe in his intoxicating woodsy scent. If she let herself get too swept up in his presence, she might not have the guts to go through with this, and she really did think it was the right move.

He handed the vase to her and held her eyes. "No, you go first."

Sam nodded and turned the faucet on as she gathered her thoughts. When the vase was three quarters full, she shut off the water and placed the flowers in. "So, an old friend showed up in town today after you left this morning." She turned to face Brent. "We went to high school together, and he owns a dealership in Dallas now."

"That's nice." Brent's left brow rose as he spoke, belaying his confusion in her statement.

"It is," Sam continued, "We got to talking, and he needs a mechanic." Understanding dawned on Brent's face, and his posture shifted. His arms folded across his chest as he leaned back. "It would just be for a few days, maybe a week." Sam shot the remaining words out in a hurry. "I can earn enough to cover the shop for a few months."

"And then what, Sam?" Brent asked. "The bill isn't going away."

Sam crossed her arms and leaned back against the counter, creating more space between them. "I know it isn't a permanent solution, but it's a solution for now. He's even putting me up in a rental house of his, so I don't have to cover rent while I'm there."

"He? Who is this guy?" Brent asked cutting her off.

Sam cringed at the harsh tone in his voice. This was not going as she expected. "I told you. He's a friend from high school."

"So, let me get this straight." Brent's eyes narrowed. "This friend from high school you haven't seen in what, a decade, shows up and offers you a job and a place to live in one of his houses and you think it's a good idea? How did he even find you?"

Sam squeezed her arms a little tighter. "He saw me, I mean us, on TV and was attending a conference near here, so he thought he'd stop by and say hi. When I told him about the shop, he offered the job." Why was Brent acting this way? While she hadn't expected him to be super excited about the time apart, she had thought he would at least understand.

"So, this guy you haven't seen in years walks in and you just tell him about your troubles? I had to practically pry it out of you. Then he offers you a job and you jump on it? I could offer you a job, Sam, and you wouldn't have to go anywhere."

Sam shook her head. Tears stung her throat but she refused to let them fall. "It's not the same. He's offering me a mechanic job. You'd be creating some job to give me money. This way I can earn it."

"Why is it so important that you earn it?"

Sam's eyes dropped to the floor. "I let Greg help me get the loan for my first shop. I think I didn't see some of the signs of his cheating because I felt like I owed him. Maybe it's stupid, but I didn't think I could break up with him while money was still owed."

"Sam, I am not Greg. I have no intentions of cheating on you." Brent grabbed her hand and she could feel the sense of urgent honesty emanating from him.

"I know you don't, but does anyone really mean to do it? I don't want the issue of money between us and I don't have any customers right now, Brent. I've been trying to figure out a way to get more - branch out into a new area or something, but I've come up short. I just need this to buy more time."

"So, you've already decided?" Brent's volume dropped to just above a whisper and the pain was evident in his voice as he said, "I thought we were in this together, Sam."

"I don't see another option, Brent, do you?" He stared at her with a pointed expression. "Other than you giving me money?"

His shoulders rose as if he were going to speak and

then fell in defeat. "No, I guess not. I just hoped we would discuss something as large as this. It's what I had planned to do."

"What do you mean?" Sam asked.

"Nothing." Brent sighed and ran a hand through his hair. "It doesn't matter now."

"Brent," Sam began, "please tell me."

He stared at her for a moment as if deciding if he wanted to share. "Julia called earlier. I was nominated for an award and they want me to attend the ceremony this next weekend. Julia suggests attending so that it keeps me relevant for when I finish the story, but I told her I needed to discuss it with you first."

"Oh." Sam's heart fell to the floor. Here Brent was asking about taking a day - true it was a day in the spotlight which would affect her as well, but she had presented her week as if it were already decided instead of asking him. She felt selfish. "Are you going to do it?"

"Well, I was hoping you would come with me if I decided to go, but it appears you'll be in Dallas."

A silence fell between them.

"I'm sorry, Brent. I should have discussed it with you instead of just deciding. I guess I've been so used to being on my own that I didn't think about it, but I really do feel it is a good move for now. Until I figure out what else to do. Will you forgive me?"

"I guess." Brent smiled. It was small, but it told Sam

he had forgiven her. "You would have hated this award show anyway. Fancy dress, getting all dolled up, etc."

Sam covered the space between them and touched his arm. "I would have done it for you, and maybe I'll finish early and be able to go with you anyway. You would still send a plane for me, right?"

"Of course." Brent held her gaze. "I'll always come for you." Then he leaned down and kissed her, and Sam's fears flew away.

# CHAPTER 21

*B*rent performed a final inspection of his Armani suit before he stepped out of the limo. It wouldn't do for him to show up in public for the first time in a month covered in lint. The driver opened the door, and Brent blinked against the flashing lights. This he didn't really miss.

He unfolded himself from the backseat and stood with a smile on his face. Attending this award show was like any other acting role. He would flash his brightest grin to appear he was enjoying himself even though his heart was miles away with Sam.

"Mr. McKasson, when are you coming out of retirement?" A voice yelled to him as he walked up the red carpet toward the entrance of the theater.

"Will there be another Night Ranger?" Another called.

"Is it true you've gotten back together with Tricia Daniels?"

Though he had ignored the rest, that one gave him pause. He was almost to the door. He should just let it go, but he didn't want it getting back to Sam.

"Actually, that one is true, isn't it darling?"

His heart stopped as he heard Tricia's voice. How had she gotten here? With a feeling of dread, he turned and she sidled up to him. Her low-cut dress left little to the imagination as it hugged her frame. To make matters worse, the dress had a slit up the thigh that reached almost to her hip. Sam would never wear something so revealing and he forced his face to remain impassive.

"What are you doing here?" he hissed out of the corner of his mouth.

"Smile." She batted her fake lashes at him. "You wouldn't want to put out a bad image, now would you?"

Anger seethed inside Brent. Tricia knew the delicate game too well. She knew he couldn't react now or the rag magazines would splash his face all over the headlines and claim he had some anger issue or pathological lying problem. His image would be ruined. "I don't know what your game is, but we are not getting back together."

In response to his cold whisper, Tricia placed a hand on his arm, threw back her head, and laughed. "You're so silly." Her voice was loud and carried to the photographers. Bulbs flashed around them.

He clenched his jaw and plastered a fake smile on his

face. With her arm linked through his, Brent led the way into the theater. As soon as the doors closed behind them, he removed her arm and turned daggers on her. "What do you think you are doing? How did you even get here?"

Tricia smiled up at him and batted her lashes again. "I guess whoever is in charge of this event still thought we were together because an invitation arrived at my house. Don't you see, Brent? It means we belong together."

"It means someone made a mistake, Tricia. That is all."

She shrugged. "Whatever. It worked in my favor. Now all the tabloids believe we are back together and as soon as your little girlfriend" - she scrunched her nose in disgust - "sees this, you'll come running back to me."

"That's where you're wrong, Tricia. Sam watches little TV and she would never watch this."

A haughty chuckle escaped Tricia's blood red lips. "Maybe not on her own, but I've paid good money to make sure she watches tonight."

Brent narrowed his eyes at her trying to make sense of her words. "What did you do?"

"Just made sure you realize we belong together."

"The only thing you've made me realize is that I should have taken a restraining order out against you long ago. Something I plan to remedy as soon as this night is over." He took a deep breath to calm the fire raging through his body. His hands curled into fists at his side, and for the first time he saw a flicker of realization spark in Tricia's eyes. "Now, get out of my sight and don't come near me the rest of the night."

Tricia opened her mouth to protest, but thought better of it. "You'll change your mind," she called as she wandered into the auditorium.

After another few deep breaths, Brent uncurled his fists. He needed to contact Sam. She was still working with Connor in Dallas, so the only way Trish could have guaranteed Sam was watching the show was if she had somehow gotten to Connor.

He extricated his cell from his pocket and punched in her number, but the phone went to voicemail. "Sam? It's Brent. I don't know exactly what Trish did, but whatever you see tonight is not the whole story. Call me as soon as you can."

His heart sank as he hung up the phone. Was it too late? Had she already seen? Surely Sam would know it was a setup, wouldn't she? But she was still recovering from a lack of trust from her last relationship, and he knew that was the one area she was still unsure about.

With a sigh, he tucked the phone back in his pocket and headed into the auditorium. There was nothing more he could do now but paste a smile on his face and pretend everything was okay.

*A* knock at the office door where Sam was working grabbed her attention. Connor stood in the doorway. "Hey, you want to get some dinner?"

She looked back over the form she was filling out. True to his word, Connor had kept her busy, not only with the used cars he had purchased but also with filling it at the shop. However, she only had a few cars left to inspect, so she figured she'd be able to return to Soda Spurs by the end of the next week. "Sure. I can finish these tomorrow."

"Great, I know of a great place." A smile lit up Connor's face and sent his blue eyes twinkling.

"As long as you understand this is not a date, Connor." While Sam appreciated the temporary job he had offered her, the last few days had been uncomfortable with Connor constantly bringing up their high school past and declaring how much he missed those times.

Connor held his hands out and ducked his head. "I promise. Just dinner."

"Fine. Let me just gather my things." Sam tucked her cell phone inside her small purse. The only contents other than her phone were her keys, wallet, and a pair of sunglasses. She was not a believer in big, bulky bags that pulled on your shoulders or whacked others when you moved in crowded places.

"Let's just take my car." Connor led her to his Mustang convertible. "I can drop you back off after dinner."

Sam hesitated not only due to the close proximity of the car but also for the inability to get away if needed, but Connor had made no move yet and it did seem silly to take two cars. "Sounds fine."

A few minutes later, Connor pulled into the parking lot of a casual restaurant. Not what Sam had been expecting, but at least it wouldn't be a candlelit dinner.

"Welcome to Charlie's," the hostess greeted them as they entered.

"Thank you. Can you sit us over there?" Connor pointed to the corner where a small secluded table sat.

Sam swallowed a sigh. It looked like he had a romantic night planned after all. At least there was a TV nearby. Maybe that could at least create a diversion.

"Of course. Follow me."

The waitress handed them menus and took their drink order before scurrying off. Sam placed her purse on the table beside her and ran her hands down her thighs. Then the awkward silence descended.

Sam cleared her throat and looked up at Connor. "I only have a few cars to finish. I should be out of your hair by Friday."

"You're not in my hair, Sam. You can stay as long as you'd like."

"I appreciate the offer, Connor, but I need to get back to Soda Spurs. I have my own shop to run."

Connor rolled his eyes. "You mean you have to get back to him, don't you? You know it will never work out between you. The two of you are too different, but you and me? We have the same interests, Sam. You could move to Dallas and be my main mechanic. We could run the dealership together."

While that once may have been a dream come true, Sam realized what she missed the most this week was home and Brent. She had thought maybe her opinion of big cities would have changed, but it hadn't. In fact, the last week had reinforced her opinion. She hated the traffic and the fact that people barely spoke to each other, much less knew each other's names.

The waitress arrived with their drinks, stalling Sam's response, but after they gave their order, Sam looked up at Connor again. "Connor, I appreciate all you've done for me. Really, I do, but I don't belong here. And I know you may not care for Brent, but I do and I miss him."

"What if he doesn't miss you?" Connor's eyes glanced up at the television screen near them.

"What are you talking about? Of course he misses me. He calls me every night."

"Must be a ruse then because it looks like he's back together with his ex. Isn't that him?"

He pointed up to the TV and Sam turned to follow his finger. Coverage of the action hero award show was one, and sure enough, there was Brent smiling on the red carpet. Sam's heart fell though as she saw the blond in the skin-tight dress on his arm. Brent said something to her and the woman laid her hand on his arm and laughed.

The smile she shot at the camera was the one of a woman in love.

Sam pushed back her chair and stood. The need to vomit surged in her stomach, and the room began to close in. She needed air. "Excuse me, I'll be right back." She scanned the area for the restroom and hurried that direction, holding onto the backs of chairs when the dizziness threatened to take over.

When she finally reached the restroom, she pushed open the door, delighted to a see a small couch in the corner. Her knees turned liquid just as she reached the couch and she fell onto it like a lead brick. How could this be happening? He knew about Greg, and he'd promised he would never do that her. Yet there he was - smiling and laughing with a done-up blond at the same award show he had invited her to. What would he have done if she had accepted his invitation? Would he have come up with some reason not to go?

Sam dropped her head onto her hands and let her shoulders shake with her tears. Connor was right. What was she doing with some billionaire who obviously hadn't given up the lifestyle yet? If the chesty blond was his type, what on earth was he doing with her? Was she just some distraction or maybe a bet with his buddies back home?

When her tears finally ceased and cold hard anger took sadness's place, Sam pushed herself up and shuffled to the sink. A look in the mirror confirmed her fears. Her eyes were red and puffy and her face was blotchy. She turned the water on and cupped her hands under the flow. Then she splashed the water on her face. After a few pats with a paper towel, Sam glanced in the mirror again. It was obvious she had been crying, but it was better. She took a deep breath and sent up a prayer for strength before returning to the table.

Their food had arrived while she was gone. Without a word, Sam sat down and bowed her head to pray over the food. When she raised her head again, Connor spoke, "Sam, I'm so sorry -"

"Stop." She shook her head at him. "I don't want to talk about it any longer tonight. We will eat and then you will take me back to my car. That is all." She knew it wasn't his fault, but she didn't want his pity. Nor did she want to encourage him to pursue her now that she was apparently single. Again. She wanted nothing to do with men at this moment, and if he were a good friend, he would understand that.

~

*B*rent checked his watch for the twentieth time that night. Time appeared to be dragging, and he really needed to get out of here and get back to Sam before he couldn't change her mind.

"And the winner of Action Hero in a Series is… Brent McKasson as Derek McCloud in the Night Ranger films."

Brent looked up at the sound of his name. Around

him, people were smiling and clapping. One woman at his table waved her hand, motioning for him to stand and take the stage. This was an amazing moment, but all Brent could think about was Sam.

On autopilot, he pushed his chair back and made his way up to the stage. He shook the presenter's hand with his right and held onto the gleaming gold statue with his left. Slowly he turned to face the crowd. As he looked over the sea of faces, he realized he didn't care about this award. He didn't even care if his book ever got published. All he wanted was Sam.

His hand darted inside his coat pocket and touched the velvet box. He knew it was fast, but he loved Sam and he had wanted to propose to her when she returned from Dallas. Now, thanks to Tricia, he wondered if that were even possible.

"You need to make your speech," the presenter whispered to him and smiled out at the audience as cameras flashed.

Suddenly, Brent had an idea. "Here, hold this." He shoved the statue back into the surprised woman's hands and pulled out the box. "First off, let me say thank you for this award. Being Derek McCloud was a high point in my life until a few months ago. Then, I met an amazing woman named Sam Jenkins. She couldn't be here tonight, but I hope she's still watching." He opened the ring case and held it up. Gasps filled the room. "Sam, I know we come from two different worlds, but that is what I love about you. You keep me grounded, and I know that I want that for the rest of my life. I'm coming for you, Sam, but I wanted you to see this, to know what's real. Will you marry me?"

He knew of course that Sam couldn't answer. Heck, she probably wasn't even still watching if she had been in the first place, but he hoped that with the cheers and clapping, the TV producers would find it newsworthy and run it several times. Everyone loved a Cinderella story; that's what Julia always said.

Brent turned back to the presenter who was dabbing at the corners of her eyes with her free hand. "That was beautiful," she sniffed. "This Sam is a lucky woman. I hope she says yes."

"Me too." Brent accepted the award from her once again and then he walked off the stage and back toward his table, but he didn't stop there. He wasn't up for any more awards and the moment was now his. Dallas and his future awaited him. He walked past the gaping mouths, pushed open the entrance doors, and stepped into the night air.

# CHAPTER 22

"Sam? Can I get you a coffee or something?"

Sam sighed and rolled her eyes. Connor had been at her office door all morning offering her coffees, muffins, massages, but she wanted none of it. She knew she looked atrocious. The dark circles around her eyes hadn't escaped her attention when she looked in the mirror this morning, but she also hadn't slept much. She'd tossed and turned most of the night as she thought about where she saw her life going now. "I'm fine, Connor. Just let me finish my work, all right?"

"I can't." He walked over to one of the chairs in the room. His hands splayed across the back and he opened his mouth to speak. Then he closed it, sighed, and shifted his weight. Something was definitely on his mind.

"What is it, Connor?" Sam had no patience for whatever game he was playing.

"I need to tell you something, but I don't want you to get mad."

"Then now is probably not the best time." Her eyes returned to the paper in hopes he would get the hint and leave, but he didn't.

"I made a mistake."

"Seems to be the trend lately."

"No, look." He tapped the back of the chair and sighed again. "Will you just come with me for a second?"

Sam rolled her eyes again and dropped the paper. She had no desire to go with him, but he clearly wasn't going to leave and let her work until she did. "Fine, what is it?"

He led the way to his office and closed the door once the two of them were inside. "Just watch. Please." Connor picked up a remote and turned on the TV that hung on his wall. A talk show filled the screen.

"Did you see that romantic proposal last night?" One of the women asked her co-host. "I don't normally swoon over things like that, but this one was…. Well, do we have footage? Let's just roll the footage."

The screen shifted then and Sam recognized Brent standing in front of a podium. A woman with dark brown hair held a gold statue next to him and an apologetic expression as if she had no idea what was happening.

"Sam, I know we come from two different worlds, but that is what I love about you. You keep me grounded, and I know that I want that for the rest of my life. I'm coming for you, Sam, but I wanted you to see this, to know what's real. Will you marry me?" He held out a box and the camera zoomed in on a beautiful diamond ring.

Confusion flooded Sam and she looked to Connor. "What, what is this?"

Connor sighed and raked a hand through his hair. "It was a setup, Sam. Tricia Daniels, his ex-girlfriend, found out we used to date. She approached me and offered me a large sum of money to get you out of the way. I've been a little underwater recently and needed the money. Plus, I really did care for you and thought if we worked together again, you might see it too."

"You took money to break up my relationship?" The room began to spin again. "What kind of person does that?"

"I'm not proud of it. And after seeing you last night and how many times Brent called-"

Sam shook her head. "Wait, what? Brent called? I haven't gotten any phone calls."

Connor bit his lip and crossed to his desk. He opened a drawer and pulled something out. "That's because you haven't had your phone." He held it out to her. "I took it while you were in the bathroom. He called you, probably as soon as he realized she had set him up. I didn't listen to the message before I deleted it, but I'm sure he was trying to tell you that what you saw with Tricia wasn't what it seemed. He's called seven times since then, though you won't see them because I deleted them all."

"You stole my phone?" How had she not noticed her

missing phone? More importantly, who was this man in front of her? Her friend from high school would never have done such an insidious thing.

His head dropped and his eyes focused on the floor. "I'm sorry, Sam. I needed the money, and I thought I would be saving you. Tricia told me he loved her, and that he'd never really leave the Hollywood life."

Sam snatched the phone from his hand as white-hot anger flared inside of her. "You had no right."

"I know, and that's why I decided to come clean today. The guilt has been eating away at me all week. The more time I spent with you, the more I wanted you to stay here, but it was wrong the way I did it."

"I don't even know what to say to you." Sam wanted to yell, to shake him, to throw something, but another part of her just wanted to curl up and cry. Was anyone real anymore?

"I understand, and you'll probably never forgive me, but perhaps you can forgive him." Connor pointed to the TV which he had paused. Brent's face still filled the screen. "He's waiting outside for you."

A barrage of conflicting emotions filled Sam. Brent was here? Sam hesitated, unsure if she wanted to see him or not.

"Go. He's got a diamond ring with your name on it, and he's not going away."

Sam spared one final glance at Connor before exiting

his office. She flung open the door only to run right into a solid chest.

"Hi Sam."

Sam stepped back and looked up into Brent's chocolate eyes. "Hi."

"I know you probably saw Tricia and I at the award ceremony, but I didn't invite her. They sent her an invitation by mistake and she caught me by surprise. I thought if I reacted the way I wanted to that it might ruin my chance at getting my story published, but I hope you also saw what happened after."

"I did." The corners of Sam's lips twitched up as happiness flooded back in. "Did you really propose to me at an award show I wasn't in attendance for?"

"I needed you to know I was serious, that I had no desire to be with Tricia. I knew she was crazy, but I didn't think she'd go this far. I filed a restraining order this morning, so she can't bother us anymore. It wasn't how I wanted to propose to you, but I didn't want to come home to find you not speaking to me or worse yet, gone."

Sam bit the inside of her lip. He knew her too well.

"So, do you have an answer for me?" Hope shone in Brent's eyes as they roamed her face.

"You can't be serious, Brent. It's too soon."

"Not for me" Brent dropped to one knee and pulled a velvet box out of his pocket. Sam gasped as he opened the lid. The ring had been beautiful on TV but it was even prettier in person. The diamond wasn't large, but it sparkled brilliantly in the middle and a row of smaller diamonds lined either side. It was perfect as she would never have wanted a large showy diamond anyway. "I was serious, Sam. I need you in my life, and I want to spend the rest of it with you. Will you marry me?"

"Yes." Sam threw her arms around Brent. "Yes, I will marry you."

EPILOGUE

*Eight Months Later*

"Okay, time to put this on." Brent held out the satin blindfold.

She smiled at him and closed her eyes. "Why exactly am I wearing a blindfold?"

"So, the surprise doesn't get ruined." With a gentle touch, he tied the cloth around her eyes and then used the opportunity to place an unexpected kiss on her lips.

"You needed to blindfold me to kiss me?" she asked with a laugh.

Brent joined in the laughter. "Oh, honey, that is not the surprise."

Sam smiled and shook her head. It had been an amazing eight months. After several conversations with Pastor Ron and a counselor, she had started working on her inability to allow people to help her. However, she and Brent had talked together and decided the shop would still lose money due to the higher rent, and they had let the lease expire.

Sam had been sad at first, but then she'd received a call from the local high school. They wanted to add Auto Shop as a class and offered Sam use of their garage, not only for classes but also for her business when there was some. She found she enjoyed teaching the next generation as much as she liked working on cars. Plus, the hours were better. She was home by four most days unless the car project was more than her students could handle and she was forced to put in extra hours. Still, she rarely worked past six and never on weekends unless it was an emergency.

Brent published his book and was getting quite a nice royalty from it. And he had another one in the works. He was making enough money that he didn't seem to miss the bigger paychecks from movie roles. Plus, he was still getting paid for the Night Ranger movies that were now in syndication. And he had brought her in on the house designs. He had already established the general layout, but as she would be living in the house too, he let her make furniture and color decisions.

They had gotten married during Christmas break when Sam was off from school, and had a short but amazing honeymoon in London.

"You've already given me enough surprises. You paid

for the wedding and then the honeymoon to London. What else do I need?"

"Just wait and see."

A few minutes later, the limo pulled to a stop. Sam heard the door open and then Brent grabbed her hand and helped her out. "Well, we're on something solid. Concrete?" Her face turned his direction as she asked the question.

He said nothing but guided her a few steps forward. Then she felt him step behind her. He pulled at the blindfold, and as it fell from her eyes, she heard a chorus of voices shout. "Surprise! Welcome home, Sam!"

"It's finished?" Sam turned questioning eyes on him.

"Yep." The house was beautiful. A sprawling four-thousand-foot ranch house with an attached three car garage and a detached shop for Sam in case the gig at the school ended.

"It's so big."

"Well, it is Texas, honey," Norma said with a laugh from the wraparound front porch.

"Aren't you going to come inside and check the rest out?" Fanny asked as she moved toward the front door.

"Yes, I suppose." Sam followed her friends inside, but her feet moved slowly as if in a daze. She had seen the skeleton of the house, but Brent hadn't let her in once it started to come together. He'd simply supplied pictures and let her work from them. Norma and Fanny took her from one room to the next, pointing out their favorite pieces. Brent followed behind, smiling at Sam as she took everything in.

Tears filled Sam's eyes at all the intricate items he had put in. Her touches were all there, combined with his. "This is too much, Brent. How will I ever repay you? There's nothing I can give you to even come close to this."

Brent's grin widened. "Actually, there is. You can give me the one thing no one else ever has."

Sam blinked at him and tried to guess what he meant. "What's that?"

"Children. The house has four rooms and I'd like to fill it."

Heat colored Sam's cheeks and her eyes dropped to the floor for a minute before meeting his gaze again. "All right, Mr. McKasson. That I can give you."

"Then I am complete." As he leaned down to kiss her, Norma, Fanny, and Paul cheered and clapped. Sam smiled and realized she finally felt completely at home.

he End!

If you would like to travel back to Soda Spurs, be sure to check out The Billionaire's Cowboy Groom.

# IT'S NOT QUITE THE END!

∼

Thank you so much for reading *A Brush With a Billionaire*. In 2017, I was privileged to be a part of Melissa Storm's Kindle World - The First Street Church. I wrote a wonderful novella called Love Breaks Through and I loved my cover because the guy on it looked like Jared Padalecki (okay, I have a little crush on him after falling in love with him first on Gilmore Girls and now on Supernatural).

However, in the summer of 2018, we received word that Amazon was shutting down the Kindle World and we were getting our rights back. Melissa offered to bring us into her publishing house or we could change the setting and release the book again ourselves. While I loved working with Melissa, I knew I had so much on my plate that it would be awhile before I would return to Sam and

Brent to do more in the series, so I decided to change and re-release. In reading through it again, I realized that Sam's and Brent's story had more to tell, so I added another 20,000 words and turned it into a novel. I thought with a little editing, I could turn Brent into a billionaire as they are all the rage right now in 2019 and Brush with a Billionaire was born.

It originally had a different cover, but when I began putting them in a series, I realized this one looked funny, so it's also had a cover change recently. It's still a fun book. I liked writing Sam as the feisty mechanic and having a town full of well-intentioned meddlers was a hoot. I have more planned for Soda Spurs, so be sure to stay tuned.

I hope you enjoyed the story as well. If you did, would you do me a favor? If you did, please leave a review. It really helps. It doesn't have to be long - just a few words to help other readers know what they're getting.

I'd love to hear from you, not only about this story, but about the characters or stories you'd like read in the future. I'm always looking for new ideas and if I use one of your characters or stories, I'll send you a free ebook and paperback of the book with a special dedication. Write to me at loranahoopes@gmail.com. And if you'd like to see what's coming next, be sure to stop by authorloranahoopes.com

I also have a weekly newsletter that contains many

wonderful things like pictures of my adorable children, chances to win awesome prizes, new releases and sales I might be holding, great books from other authors, and anything else that strikes my fancy and that I think you would enjoy. I'll even send you the first chapter of my newest (maybe not even released yet) book if you'd like to sign up.

Even better, I solemnly swear to only send out one newsletter a week (usually on Tuesday unless life gets in the way which with three kids it usually does). I will not spam you, sell your email address to solicitors or anyone else, or any of those other terrible things.

And if you're interested in meeting the rest of the billionaires in the series, be sure to check out The Billionaire's Christmas Miracle. Turn the page for a sneak peek.

# NOT READY TO SAY GOODBYE YET?

Sam and Brent will appear just briefly in book 4, but I do plan to revisit Soda Spurs again. Until that time though, I'd love to introduce you to Drew and Gwen.

## The Billionaire's Christmas Miracle

**He's a billionaire tired of the elite life...**

Drew Devonshire owns a chain of hotels with his family, but he wants more out of life. His curiosity is piqued when he meets a mysterious stranger at a masquerade party.

**She never meant to deceive him...**

but when her friend asks her to pretend to be her at a party, Gwen doesn't see the harm. Until she meets Drew Devonshire. Now, he wants to pursue her, but can she tell him who she really is?

**Will a mistaken identity....**

keep them from finding love?

Read on for a taste of The Billionaire's Christmas Miracle....

## THE BILLIONAIRE'S CHRISTMAS MIRACLE PREVIEW

Gwen's jaw dropped as she regarded her friend. Surely, she had misheard Carrie's request. There was no way she could be serious. "You want me to do what?" Didn't Carrie understand what she was asking was one of Gwen's worst nightmares?

"Pretend to be me." Carrie flicked her fiery red hair off her shoulder and picked up the eyeshadow brush. She swiped it across her lid, nonchalantly, as if she had just been asking Gwen to hand her a shirt and not walk into a room full of strangers. Strangers!

"Just for the night. I'm so tired of these parties, and I promised Lorenzo I'd go riding with him." Lorenzo was Carrie's latest fling - a tall, dark, Italian bad boy who wore leather and drove a Harley. At least Gwen was fairly certain his name was Lorenzo. Carrie Bliss changed men like most people changed socks, and she had a hard time keeping up.

While Gwen adored Carrie, she often wondered how they were still friends. In college, it had made sense. Gwen was the studious library aide and Carrie was the sorority girl who needed help on her papers. But now? Carrie owned her own business and was steadily climbing the "Who's who in society" ladder while Gwen was an ordinary English teacher. A teacher who had nightmares every year about meeting the upcoming class of students, but they were just kids. Kids like she had been once who needed help, so she could swallow her fear of strangers and stand up in front of them, but she could not walk into a party with a bunch of wealthy adults. Carrie knew this.

"But we don't look alike," Gwen protested with a shake of her head. That wasn't exactly true. They had been mistaken for sisters more than once, but she needed an excuse. Any excuse.

Carrie set the make-up down and turned to Gwen. Her right eyebrow inched up her forehead in a stop-being-a-baby expression. "We look close enough. We both have red hair, we're about the same height-"

"You're two sizes smaller than me," Gwen finished. She wasn't overweight, but her size eight to ten frame was bigger than Carrie's perfect size six one.

Carrie flashed her manicured hand in a dismissive wave. French tips. They were so pretty. Gwen's own nails were all different lengths and not painted. She'd only had one manicure in her life. High school prom. Her foster mother had taken her to get a manicure even though she didn't have a date. "Everyone should feel pretty at least one day," she'd said. Carrie, on the other hand, had a weekly standing appointment with her nail lady, and while she'd offered to take Gwen along and pay for hers more than once, Gwen just couldn't do it. It seemed like a frivolous waste of money even if it wasn't her money.

"Just don't get too close to anyone, and no one will know. Besides, most of these people barely know me. They just know the name of Carrie Bliss Designs. The only one you'd have to watch out for is Grant." Her nose wrinkled the tiniest bit as she said his name.

Grant was Carrie's ex - a snobby stock broker who managed the portfolios of many of the wealthiest in the city. Gwen had never liked Grant nor understood why Carrie dated him, but then again, she didn't understand why Carrie dated half the men she did. "I don't know, Carrie, it's not really my thing."

"Which is exactly why you should go." Carrie turned back to the mirror and puckered her lips. "You never do anything fun. You go to work and then you come home and hang out there."

That part was true; Gwen's life was boring, but she liked it that way. At least most days. "I'm a homebody. I like staying home." Plus, it was safer there. No one would beat her or die on her if she stayed in her house. Yes, it was lonely on occasion, but still safer.

Carrie's eyes flicked up to catch Gwen's in the mirror. "But you'll never meet anyone stuck inside this house."

Which was the whole point. Gwen didn't want to meet someone. It hurt too much to love people.

"Besides, this is the perfect opportunity," Carrie continued, "you'll be wearing a mask, so you can hide behind it."

Gwen's teeth bit into her bottom lip. Wearing the mask might make it better. It wouldn't curb her anxiety about being in a room full of strangers, but it would help that they couldn't really see her. And it would be something different. "What will I wear?" Gwen couldn't believe she was even considering this. "Is it formal? Because I have nothing formal."

"Relax, I'm sure I have something in my closet that will fit you. Come on, let's go look."

She followed Carrie to her immense closet. Though they had shared an apartment for a time in college, eventually Carrie's more expensive taste and wallet had led her to purchase a penthouse in the city. Gwen, however, rented a studio in a much poorer section of town.

"Let's see." Carrie walked along the dresses hanging down, her hand touching each garment as she passed. Gwen would never get used to the size of this closet. It was nearly the size of her whole apartment. Carrie stopped and pulled out an emerald green gown. "Try this one. I remember it being slightly big on me, so it's probably just your size."

Gwen's fingers touched the satiny gown. It was more expensive than anything she would ever own. Off the shoulder and floor length, the satin rippled like waves as it fell to the floor. "What if I ruin it?" Gwen wasn't exactly a klutz, but she could just picture herself spilling a fancy drink on the beautiful gown.

Carrie smiled. "You won't, and even if you do, it's not like I'm hurting for it." She gestured to the myriad of dresses still hanging on the rods.

She was running out of excuses, and it was just one night. Perhaps it would even be fun, and she could reminisce on the evening later when the silence pressed in on her at her apartment. It wasn't like she would have another chance at something like this. "Okay, I'll see if it fits."

Carrie stepped out of the closet to give Gwen some privacy. She laid the gown across the padded bench and shook her head. Who had a bench in their closet? She didn't think she would ever get used to some of the things wealthy people seemed to waste their money on.

Her fingers trembled slightly as she removed her clothes and stepped into the dress. *This is wrong* paraded again and again in her head like a scratched record, but her hands still pulled the dress up. Her fingers still found the zipper and tugged. It was a little snug, but it fit. If she didn't eat too much.

Lifting the dress so as not to step on the hem, Gwen stepped out of the closet. Carrie clapped her hands and sighed. "Yes, you look perfect. Well, almost perfect. Hang on." She hurried back into the closet and the sound of drawers opening and closing carried out. "Ah, here we go." She re-emerged holding a feathered mask and held it out. "Now, you'll look perfect."

Gwen's fingers grasped the mask, a beautiful atrocity of purples, greens, and golds. She pulled the string and fastened it over her face before turning to the mirror. Whoa! Her lips parted at the vision in front of her, and a small gasp escaped. She looked... beautiful, and Carrie was right - no one would know it wasn't Carrie from far away. With her face covered, she appeared even more like her friend.

"See? I told you. Now let's get you some shoes, a little jewelry, and pin your hair up."

Gwen glanced down at her wrist. "Can I keep the bracelet on at least?" It was the last thing her parents had given her - a diamond tennis bracelet. And it never came off, not even to shower.

Carrie's eyes softened. She had never met Gwen's parents - they had been dead for years before Carrie entered the picture, but Gwen had told her about them one late night over popcorn and The Breakfast Club. "I'd never ask you to take your bracelet off. I was just thinking some diamond earrings would be a great match with it."

Tears filled Gwen's eyes. *This* was why she and Carrie

were still friends. Though worlds apart, she was so thoughtful sometimes.

With the earrings picked and the shoes found, Gwen checked the mirror one last time. She still couldn't believe she was doing this, but she might as well make the most of it. For one night, she could pretend to be Carrie, pretend to be wanted, pretend to be wealthy and not have a care in the world. It was just one night.

~

*D*rew Devonshire adjusted his mask. He looked a little like the Phantom with his white shirt, dark pants, and cape, but the look suited him. If only he were more excited about this event, but they were all the same. He'd been attending them for years, and the results never changed. By the end of the night, he would be dying of boredom, dazed from the alcohol he'd consumed to battle said boredom, and have at least a dozen numbers in his pocket from women after his money whom he had no interest in.

It was always the same people there - the affluent and elite of society. They would gather at some elaborate venue with tiny portions of intricate food that would cost whoever was hosting the event a fortune. In this case, that was Drew, or his family rather, as his mother was hosting this masquerade ball at one of their hotels.

Occasionally, a millionaire from another town would

be in attendance or sometimes a relative of one of the families would be, but even those instances were rare. His mother invited old friends and only new people she thought would attend her next benefit. Since those were priced at a thousand dollars a plate that list was small. Plus, while the food was delectable, it never filled him up, and he invariably had to have his chef make him a second meal when he returned home.

If only he could get out of this, but his mother would be there. If he didn't attend, she would be livid. As heir to the billion-dollar hotel chain, it was his duty to attend events like this. Maybe he could leave early, but what would he do even if he could? Return home to his mansion and watch television alone again? He already did that nightly.

For a time, he had filled his nights with women. One after the other, he had wined them and dined them, but none had held his interest. Soon, the very thought of dating and pretending to like them had grown old. They were all alike - cookie cutters of their mothers and their mothers before them. Tailored clothing, designer shoes, and an appetite for spending money without abandonment appeared to be all that drove these women. Drew wanted something different. He had no idea what, but something different. No, that wasn't true. He wanted someone like Marjorie had been or who he thought Marjorie had been.

A knock sounded on his door. "Come in." It had to be

Pierre, his butler. Though officially the help, Pierre felt more like family. He had been Drew's butler for over a decade now and his confidante almost as long.

"Are you ready, sir? Manuel has the limo waiting." Pierre was older than Drew, gray at the temples and with more lines on his face, but still handsome. He had never wanted to marry, and as Drew paid him well, he seemed content to remain Drew's main butler, but he had a few men beneath him, so he could take time off when he needed.

Drew sighed. It wasn't as if he had much choice. "I suppose I am." He shoved his wallet in his pocket. "Pierre, is there anything else going on tonight? If I finish early?"

Pierre's brows knitted together. "Early, sir? Don't these events run on the lengthy side?"

"Yes, they do, but I was thinking about retiring early." He hoped Pierre was catching his innuendo. "If something else were going on that sounded interesting, I mean."

Pierre nodded. "Ah, I see. I'm afraid I am not well informed on the night life around town, but Manuel usually has knowledge of such events. Although I must say, the Devonshire events are always the talk of the town, so I'm not sure what else you might be looking for."

That elicited a small smile from Drew. He clapped Pierre on the shoulder. "Me either, but thank you, my friend. I will ask Manuel."

"Very good, sir." Pierre nodded and stepped out of the way, so Drew could exit the room.

Though he lived alone, except for the help he employed, his mansion was palatial. Five bedrooms each with their own bathroom took up the second floor. A large grandiose stairway connected the two floors, and his loafers clicked against the white marble as he made his way down them.

The stairs ended in the grand foyer, a room as large as most people's living rooms with the sole purpose of connecting the front door to the living room. A single closet to hang coats in and a hat rack which held his hat and scarf were the only things in the room besides a mirror that hung on one wall.

After donning his hat and wrapping his scarf around his neck, Drew checked his reflection in this mirror. The image reflecting back was dapper if he did say so himself. He flung open the front door to find Manuel waiting on the porch.

"Are you ready, sir?" Manuel was much younger than Pierre. Younger than Drew even, but he'd come highly recommended after Drew's last driver had run off with Marjorie. And so far, Drew had no complaints. Manuel always dressed immaculately, he drove the speed limit, and he kept the limo stocked with Drew's favorite snacks - beef jerky and Doritos.

Not the typical fare for a billionaire, but then Drew wasn't the typical billionaire. He didn't like the taste of

Dom Perignon, and caviar held no appeal for him either. While the help and the limo were nice, sometimes he wished he could just go camping in the woods with some burger patties, hot dogs, and chips.

His mother hated that side of him. "We should never have allowed you to go off to a regular college," she reminded him often, but Drew was glad he'd gotten the chance to see how the other half lived. In fact, he'd wanted to do something other than inherit a billion-dollar hotel industry, but when his father died, he'd been forced to step into his shoes.

"As ready as I'll ever be, I suppose," Drew said as he followed Manuel to the long black car.

Manuel nodded as if he understood what Drew meant though Drew knew he did not understand. People thought they wanted to be wealthy, but they had no idea the taxing monotony it carried with it. He always had to be dressed when he went outside. One poorly chosen outfit and his face would end up splashed across the tabloids within hours. Dates needed to be well planned out, and he could never say what he was thinking. Having to always be diplomatic required constant attention and control. And Drew was tired of it.

Plus, there was the prying into his private life. After Marjorie had run away with the chauffeur, he had been the talk of every tabloid. It was only after a fellow heiress had gotten herself arrested for driving intoxicated that he had faded from the public scrutiny and pity.

"Manuel, if I wanted to leave the ball early, would you know of any place that might have something of interest going on tonight?"

Manuel pursed his lips. "Do you mean of the local nightlife variety?"

Drew slid into the leather seat and nodded. "That is precisely what I mean."

"I have heard nothing other than the talk of this masquerade ball."

Drew sighed. Of course, he hadn't. Drew's mother did her best to make sure her parties conflicted with nothing and garnered all the attention. "I was afraid of that, but do me a favor, will you, Manuel? Keep your ears open in case something comes up."

Manuel nodded. "I will do my best, sir." Then he shut the door and Drew was left alone in the dimly lit interior of the limo.

Continue reading The Billionaire's Christmas Miracle...

Or get the boxed set with all 4 books and save 38%

## A FREE STORY FOR YOU

~

*E*njoyed this story? Not ready to quit reading yet? If you sign up for my newsletter, you will receive The Billionaire's Impromptu Bet right away as my thank you gift for choosing to hang out with me.

## The Billionaire's Impromptu Bet

**A SWAT officer. A bored billionaire heiress. A bet that could change everything....**

Read on for a taste of The Billionaire's Impromptu Bet....

# THE BILLIONAIRE'S IMPROMPTU BET
## PREVIEW

*B*rie Carter fell back spread eagle on her queen-sized canopy bed sending her blond hair fanning out behind her. With a large sigh, she uttered, "I'm bored."

"How can you be bored? You have like millions of dollars." Her friend, Ariel, plopped down in a seated position on the bed beside her and flicked her raven hair off her shoulder. "You want to go shopping? I hear Tiffany's is having a special right now."

Brie rolled her eyes. Shopping? Where was the excitement in that? With her three platinum cards, she could go shopping whenever she wanted. "No, I'm bored with shopping too. I have everything. I want to do something exciting. Something we don't normally do."

Brie enjoyed being rich. She loved the unlimited credit cards at her disposal, the constant apparel of new clothes, and of course the penthouse apartment her father paid for, but lately, she longed for something more fulfilling.

Ariel's hazel eyes widened. "I know. There's a new bar down on Franklin Street. Why don't we go play a little game?"

Brie sat up, intrigued at the secrecy and the twinkle in Ariel's eyes. "What kind of game?"

"A betting game. You let me pick out any man in the place. Then you try to get him to propose to you."

Brie wrinkled her nose. "But I don't want to get married." She loved her freedom and didn't want to share her penthouse with anyone, especially some man.

"You don't marry him, silly. You just get him to propose."

Brie bit her lip as she thought. It had been awhile since her last relationship and having a man dote on her for a month might be interesting, but…. "I don't know. It doesn't seem very nice."

"How about I sweeten the pot? If you win, I'll set you up on a date with my brother."

Brie cocked her head. Was she serious? The only thing Brie couldn't seem to buy in the world was the affection of Ariel's very handsome, very wealthy, brother. He was a movie star, just the kind of person Brie could consider marrying in the future. She'd had a crush on him as long as she and Ariel had been friends, but he'd always seen her as just that, his little sister's friend. "I thought you didn't want me dating your brother."

"I don't." Ariel shrugged. "But he's between girlfriends right now, and I know you've wanted it for ages. If you win this bet, I'll set you up. I can't guarantee any more than one date though. The rest will be up to you."

Brie wasn't worried about that. Charm she possessed in abundance. She simply needed some alone time with him, and she was certain she'd be able to convince him they were meant to be together. "All right. You've got a deal."

Ariel smiled. "Perfect. Let's get you changed then and see who the lucky man will be.

A tiny tug pulled on Brie's heart that this still wasn't right, but she dismissed it. This was simply a means to an end, and he'd never have to know.

~

*J*esse Calhoun relaxed as the rhythmic thudding of the speed bag reached his ears. Though he loved his job, it was stressful being the SWAT sniper. He hated having to take human lives and today had been especially rough. The team had been called out to a drug bust, and Jesse was forced to return fire at three hostiles. He didn't care that they fired at his team and himself first. Taking a life was always hard, and every one of them haunted his dreams.

"You gonna bust that one too?" His co-worker Brendan appeared by his side. Brendan was the opposite of Jesse in nearly every way. Where Jesse's hair was a dark copper, Brendan's was nearly black. Jesse sported paler skin and a dusting of freckles across his nose, but Brendan's skin was naturally dark and freckle free.

Jesse flashed a crooked grin, but kept his eyes on the small, swinging black bag. The speed bag was his way to release, but a few times he had started hitting while still too keyed up and he had ruptured the bag. Okay, five times, but who was counting really? Besides, it was a better way to calm his nerves than other things he could choose. Drinking, fights, gambling, women.

"Nah, I think this one will last a little longer." His shoulders began to burn, and he gave the bag another few punches for good measure before dropping his arms and letting it swing to a stop. "See? It lives to be hit at least another day." Every once in a while, Jesse missed training the way he used to. Before he joined the force, he had been an amateur boxer, on his way to being a pro, but a shoulder injury had delayed his training and forced him to consider something else. It had eventually healed, but by then he had lost his edge.

"Hey, why don't you come drink with us?" Brendan clapped a hand on Jesse's shoulder as they headed into the locker room.

"You know I don't drink." Jesse often felt like the outsider of the team. While half of the six-man team was married, the other half found solace in empty bottles and meaningless relationships. Jesse understood that - their job was such that they never knew if they would come home night after night - but he still couldn't partake.

Brendan opened his locker and pulled out a clean shirt. He peeled off his current one and added deodorant before tugging on the new one. "You don't have to drink. Look, I won't drink either. Just come and hang out with us. You have no one waiting for you at home."

That wasn't entirely true. Jesse had Bugsy, his Boston Terrier, but he understood Brendan's point. Most days, Jesse went home, fed Bugsy, made dinner, and fell asleep watching TV on the couch. It wasn't much of a life. "All right, I'll go, but I'm not drinking."

Brendan's lips pulled back to reveal his perfectly white teeth. He bragged about them, but Jesse knew they were veneers. "That's the spirit. Hurry up and change. We don't want to leave the rest of the team waiting."

"Is everyone coming?" Jesse pulled out his shower necessities. Brendan might feel comfortable going out with just a new application of deodorant, but Jesse needed to wash more than just dirt and sweat off. He needed to wash the sound of the bullets and the sight of lifeless bodies from his mind.

"Yeah, Pat's wife is pregnant again and demanding some crazy food concoctions. Pat agreed to pick them up if she let him have an hour. Cam and Jared's wives are having a girls' night, so the whole gang can be together. It will be nice to hang out when we aren't worried about being shot at."

"Fine. Give me ten minutes. Unlike you, I like to clean up before I go out."

Brendan smirked. "I've never had any complaints. Besides, do you know how long it takes me to get my hair like this?"

Jesse shook his head as he walked into the shower, but he knew it was true. Brendan had rugged good looks and muscles to match. He rarely had a hard time finding a woman. Jesse on the other hand hadn't dated anyone in the last few months. It wasn't that he hadn't been looking, but he was quieter than his teammates. And he wasn't looking for right now. He was looking for forever. He just hadn't found it yet.

Click here to continue reading The Billionaire's Impromptu Bet.

# THE STORY DOESN'T END!

You've met a few people and fallen in love....

I bet you're wondering how you can meet everyone else.

**Star Lake Series:**

**When Love Returns:** The first in the Star Lake series. Presley Hays and Brandon Scott were best friends in High School until Morgan entered their town and stole Brandon's heart. Devastated, Presley takes a scholarship to Le Cordon Bleu, but five years later, she is back in Star Lake after a tough breakup. Brandon thought he'd never return to Star Lake after Morgan left him and his daughter Joy, but when his father needs help, he returns home and finds more than he bargained for. Can Presley and Brandon forget past hurts or will their stubborn natures keep them apart forever?

**Once Upon a Star:** The second book in the Star Lake series. Audrey left Star Lake to pursue acting, but after an unplanned pregnancy her jobs and her money dwindled, leaving her no option except to return home and start over. Blake was the quintessential nerd in high school and was never able to tell Audrey how he felt. Now that he's gained confidence and some muscle, will he finally be able to reveal his feelings? Once Upon a Star will take you back to Christmas in Star Lake. Revisit your favorite characters and meet a few ones in this sweet Christmas read.

**Love Conquers All:** Lanie Perkins Hall never imagined being divorced at thirty. Nor did she imagine falling for an old friend, but when she runs into Azarius Jacobson, she can't deny the attraction. As they begin to spend more time together, Lanie struggles with the fact Azarius keeps his past a secret. What is he hiding? And will she ever be able to get him to open up? Azarius Jacobson has loved Lanie Perkins Hall from the moment he saw her, but issues from his past have left him guarded. Now that he has another chance with her, will he find the courage to share his life with her? Or will his emotional walls create a barrier that will leave him alone once more? Find out in this heartfelt, emotional third book (stand alone) in the Star Lake series.

**The Heartbeats Series:**

**Where It All Began:** Sandra Baker thought her life was on the right track until she ended up pregnant. Her boyfriend, not wanting the baby, pushes her to have an abortion. After the procedure, Sandra's life falls apart, and she turns to alcohol. Her relationship ends, and she struggles to find meaning in her life. When she meets Henry Dobbs, a strong Christian man, she begins to wonder if God would accept her. Will she tell Henry her darkest secret? And will she ever be able to forgive herself and find healing? Find out in this emotional love story.

**The Power of Prayer:** Callie Green thought she had her whole life planned out until her fiance left her at the altar. When her carefully laid plans crumble, she begins to make mistakes at work and engage in uncharacteristic activities. After a mistake nearly costs her her job, she cashes in her honeymoon tickets for some time away. There she meets JD, a charming Christian man who, even though she is not a believer, captures her interest. Before their relationship can deepen, Callie's ex-fiance shows back up in her life and she is forced to choose between Daniel and JD. Who will she choose and how will her choice affect the rest of her life? Find out in this touching novel.

**When Hearts Collide:** Amanda Adams has always been a Christian, but she's a novice at relationships. When she meets Caleb, her emotions get the best of her and she ignores the sign that something is amiss. Will she find out before it's too late? Jared Masterson is still healing from his girlfriend's strange rejection and disappearance when he meets Amanda. She captivates his heart, but can he save her from making the biggest mistake of her life? A must read for mothers and daughters. Though part of the series and the first of the college spin off series, it is a stand alone book and can be read separately.

**A Past Forgiven:** Jess Peterson has lived a life of abuse and lost her self worth, but when she is paired with a Christian roommate, she begins to wonder if there is a loving father looking down on her. Her decisions lead her one way, but when she ends up pregnant, she must make some major changes. Chad Michelson is healing from his own past and uses meaningless relationships to hide his pain, but when Jess becomes pregnant, he begins to wonder about the meaning of life. Can he step up and be there for Jess and the baby?

**Sweet Billionaires Series:**

**The Billionaire's Secret:** Maxwell Banks was the ultimate player until he found himself caring for a daughter he didn't know he had. Can he change to become the role model she needs? Alyssa Miller hasn't had the best luck with past relationships, so why is she falling for the one man who is sure to break her heart? Though nearly complete opposites, feelings develop, but can Max really change his philandering ways? Or will one mistake seal his fate forever?

**A Brush with a Billionaire:** Brent just wanted to finish his novel in peace, but when his car breaks down in Sweet Grove, he is forced to deal with a female mechanic and try to get along. Sam thought she had given up on city boys, but when Brent shows up in her shop, she finds herself fighting attraction. Will their stubborn natures keep them apart or can a small town festival bring them together?

**The Billionaire's Christmas Miracle:** Drew Devonshire is captivated by the woman he meets at a masquerade ball, but who is she? Gwen Rodgers is a teacher, but when she pretends to be her friend and meets Drew at a masquerade ball, her world gets thrown upside down.

**The Billionaire's Cowboy Groom:** Carrie Bliss finally found the man she wants to marry but there's just one little problem. She's technically still married. Cal Roper hasn't seen her in years but his heart still belongs to his wife. When she returns to town requesting a divorce, can he convince her they belong together?

**The Cowboy Billionaire: Coming Soon!**

**The Lawkeeper Series:**

**Lawfully Matched:** Kate Whidby doesn't want to impose on her newly married brother after their parents die, so she accepts a mail order bride offer in the paper. Little does she know the man she intends to marry has a dark past, sending her fleeing into a neighboring town and into Jesse Jenning's life. Jesse never wanted to be in law enforcement, but after a band of robbers kills his fiancee, he dons the badge and swears revenge. Will he find his fiancee's killer? And when Kate flies into his life, will he be able to put his painful past behind him in order to love again?

**Lawfully Justified:** William Cook turns to bounty hunting after losing his wife. When he suffers a life-threatening injury, he is forced to stay in town with an intriguing woman. Emma Stewart has moved back in with her widowed father, the town doctor, but she still longs for a family of her own, so no one is more surprised than she is when she starts to develop feeling for the bounty hunter, who hides his heart of gold behind a rugged exterior. Can Emma offer William a reason to stay? Can William find a way to heal from his broken past to start a future with Emma? Or will a haunting secret take away all the possibilities of this budding romance?

**The Scarlet Wedding:** William and Emma are planning their wedding, but an outbreak and a return from his past force them to change their plans. Is a happily ever after still in their future?

**Lawfully Redeemed:** Dani Higgins is a K9 cop looking to make a name for herself, but she finds herself at the mercy of a stranger after an accident. Calvin Phillips just wanted to help his brother, but somehow he ended up in the middle of a police investigation and caring for the woman trying to bring his brother in.

**The Still Small Voice Series:**

**The Still Small Voice:** Jordan Wright was searching for something after she gave her son up for adoption. What she found was God, and she began receiving visions. But can she trust Him when he asks her to do something big? Kat Jameson had long been a lukewarm Christian, but when her friend dies and she begins seeing lights, she thinks she is going crazy. Then she meets someone with a message for her. Will she be able to give up control and do what is asked of her?

**A Spark in the Darkness** coming soon!

**Blushing Brides Series:**

**The Cowboy's Reality Bride:** Tyler Hall just wanted to find love, but the women he dated wanted more than his small-town life provided. He gets more than he bargained for when he ends up on a reality dating show and falls for a woman who is not a contestant. Laney Swann has been running from her past for years, but it takes meeting a man on a reality dating show to make her see there's no need to run.

**The Reality Bride's Baby:** Laney wants nothing more than a baby, but when she starts feeling dizzy is it pregnancy or something more serious?

**The Producer's Unlikely Bride:** Justin Miller had

given up on love, but when his image needs help, he finds himself needing the aid of a stranger who just happens to be a romance writer. Ava McDermott is waiting for the perfect love, but after agreeing to a fake relationship with Justin, she finds herself falling for real.

**Ava's Blessing in Disguise:** Five years after marriage, Ava faces a mysterious illness that threatens to ruin her career. Will she find out what it is?

**The Soldier's Steadfast Bride: coming soon**

**The Men of Fire Beach**

**Fire Games:** Cassidy returns home from Who Wants to Marry a Cowboy to find obsessive letters from a fan. The cop assigned to help her wants to get back to his case, but what she sees at a fire may just be the key he's looking for.

**Lost Memories and New Beginnings: coming soon**

**Stand Alones:**

**Love Renewed:** This books is part of the multi author second chance series. When fate reunites high school sweethearts separated by life's choices, can they find a second chance at love at a snowy lodge amid a little mystery?

Her children's early reader chapter book series:

The Wishing Stone #1: Dangerous Dinosaur

The Wishing Stone #2: Dragon Dilemma
The Wishing Stone #3: Mesmerizing Mermaids
The Wishing Stone #4: Pyramid Puzzle
The Wishing Stone Inspirations 1: Mary's Miracle
To see a list of all her books

authorloranahoopes.com
loranahoopes@gmail.com

# ABOUT THE AUTHOR

Lorana Hoopes is an inspirational author originally from Texas but now living in the PNW with her husband and three children. When not writing, she can be seen kickboxing at the gym, singing, or acting on stage. One day, she hopes to retire from teaching and write full time.